All rights reserved.
ISBN - 13: 978-1998775606
Give feedback on the book at:
lorhainneeckhart@hotmail.com

Twitter: @LEckhart
Facebook: AuthorLorhainneEckhart

Printed in the U.S.A

The One

THE WILDE BROTHERS
BOOK ONE

LORHAINNE ECKHART

She's lost everything. He believes she's despised him all his life. A tragic mistake could be their only redemption. *"Get the book one reader called "the perfect recipe for an awesome story that will have you on edge from start to finish"*

"Showing strength but vulnerabilities in characters is not easy to do well, but Ms Eckhart does it exceedingly well."

REVIEWER, BJ NORTON

"Margaret is a failed surgeon who is running from her past. Enter Joe Wilde a handsome father of a troubled fourteen year old boy, Ryan. Rich with a western flavor, high drama and romance that satisfies, this book is a definite winner.

KELSEY TANNER

"Once again Lorhainne has captured me in her writings. A wonderful book, just like the books about the Friessen men. This series is going to be just as good."

The Wilde Brothers

Come and meet the Wilde Brothers of Idaho. Joe, Logan, Ben, Samuel, and Jake. You'll love the western flair and hot men and strong women in this romantic family saga.

The One
The Honeymoon
Friendly Fire
A Matter of Trust
The Reckoning
Traded
Unforgiven
The Holiday Bride

A passionate and stirring love story: After losing her job as a surgeon, Margaret retreats to her hometown — where she runs into Joe Wilde, the man she's wanted for years.

In THE ONE, Margaret Gordon was once a prominent Seattle surgeon, and after an accident returns to her hometown, the perfect spot to hide out from everyone and to lick her wounds, with no one around but her horse.

Margaret never considered herself a horse person. But when the now-widowed Joe Wilde drives in one morning with a teenage boy and a horse with a problem, Margaret turns into that klutzy teenage misfit that silently carried a torch for Joe all through school. But when smooth-talking Joe convinces Margaret into working with the temperamental horse, sparks fly and sizzle between them. Only Joe believes Margaret has despised him all his life, and when life throws Joe a curveball he soon finds out the right woman he's been looking for has been there all along.

Can Joe and Margaret put aside their differences and realize that the other is, The One?

CHAPTER
One

Margaret Gordon leaned against the splintered front steps, watching the sun rise from the privacy of her front yard. There were only two things that could have irritated her as she stood outside the older two-bedroom farmhouse she'd inherited from her grandfather—which she still found odd, him leaving everything to her and not her mother, who felt slighted. The first thing was the possibility of having her morning coffee interrupted by anyone, and the second was the sight of an uninvited guest, driving a dark blue truck spewing dust and gravel down her very private driveway.

The large four by four pulled in, stopping a few feet in front of her. Margaret froze. Instead of turning, running back into the house and slamming the door, she found herself rooted to the spot, suffering a sudden lapse of basic social skills. Her eyes widened, and she stared in horror as a tall, dark-haired man dressed in a tan barn coat and blue jeans stepped out of the truck. His wavy hair was a little shaggy, falling just past his ears and flickering almost black under the early morning sunlight. He was handsome, with a square jaw and the kind of body a woman would never tire of…and he was staring at her now with an unusual amount of interest.

When the passenger door slammed, Margaret jumped, spilling what was left of her coffee on the wrinkled jeans she'd pulled on that morning. "Shit…" she muttered, biting her tongue before she could embarrass herself further. She wiped the wet spot on her pants before fisting her hand and giving up. A tall, gangly boy fell in behind the cowboy. Obviously, they were father and son, but what did the pair want with her? Margaret yanked down her wide-brimmed cowboy hat and yanked up the collar of her grandfather's old wool coat. She'd just climbed out of bed and hadn't taken the time to splash water on her face or run a brush through her long, dark hair. Her first priority had been coffee, outside, in this cool April morning on her very private twenty acres that no one ever visited. She was horrified. For a minute, she wondered if she smelled, and then she worried about how bad she looked.

Margaret wished she was sitting down as she lowered her gaze, fighting the urge to press her hand over her pounding heart. She dumped out the rest of her coffee, creating a puddle at her feet, and then stared at the tall man, all muscles and arrogance, striding toward her.

"I'm looking for a Miss Gordon," he barked.

"You found her. What can I do for you?" Margaret didn't move, nor did she offer—in any neighborly kind of way—a cup of coffee, a hello, or any sort of welcome.

"Mister Jerow at the feed store mentioned you do some work with horses," the man said.

Margaret watched as he stepped closer still, but the gangly boy beside him took one look at her and hung back. She guessed that was her answer: without grabbing a mirror, she knew she looked rough and untidy. She frowned. The kid appeared scared of his own shadow or, she supposed, her prickly attitude. Scaring kids was not something she wanted to be known for. As it was, Margaret Gordon, former neurosurgeon from Seattle, was already known for destroying kids' futures. At least that was how she saw herself, anyway.

"You do work with horses, don't you?" he said. He had a deep, smoky voice that rattled her insides.

Margaret stared at him, thinking there was something seriously wrong with her to be so affected by some back-woods cowboy, and then shook her head. "Don't know why Mister Jerow would have told you that," she said. Though the truth was, that since Margaret had returned to Post Falls, Idaho, in a haze of shame, she was more comfortable with animals than she was with people, because animals didn't lie.

The man looked away, confused, and let out a harsh chuckle. "Sorry to have wasted your time," he said. Her horse nickered from the rough bark corral her grandfather had built from the trees on the land. "That your horse?" the man asked as he wandered closer to Angel, her five-year-old Egyptian Arabian.

Margaret couldn't believe how he walked right up to Angel and stroked her with his large hand. Angel never lets anyone near her except Margaret, and she nickered again as the man touched her forelock and rubbed her neck, turning heavenly blue eyes on Margaret. Her stomach flip-flopped and her cheeks burned. Out of the corner of her eye, she glimpsed the awkward teen, who wore baggy jeans and a dark hoodie, with the same dark hair as the man who leaned against her corral. The teen wore a baseball cap over hair long enough to cover his ears, and he shuffled his scuffed sneakers, kicking up the dust. He dropped his gaze to the ground.

"You don't talk much, do you?" the man said from where he leaned over by her horse.

"I already told you I can't help you," she snapped, swinging her favorite mug and wishing she could slip back into the house and shut the door. Why wouldn't they just leave?

"I don't think you really answered me," the man replied.

She couldn't believe it—the man was smiling at her. What made it worse was that he had one of those million-dollar smiles, with a set of dimples that had her legs softening to limp noodles.

"What are you looking for?" She tried to cross her arms but was hampered by the cracked mug she held. She felt like an idiot.

"My boy's horse, he can't get near it. Forget riding it. Told him unless we can find someone to straighten the horse out, I'm getting rid of it. I'm not paying to feed a dangerous animal that's of no use to me."

Margaret watched the boy's face hardening as his father spoke. A glimmer of hurt flashed in the teen's eyes. She recognized that tough, pain-in-the-ass, don't-give-a-crap attitude written all over the kid's face. It was the same expression she had worn as a twelve-year-old tomboy sent to live with her grandfather, Carl Spick, by a corporate mother busy fast-tracking her career as a top-ten stockbroker in Seattle. Being unwanted and considered a nuisance had produced all kinds of attitude and a profound, deep hurt in Margaret. What was this kid's story?

"That true, kid?" she asked the boy.

The kid jerked his head up and stared at her, wide

eyed. He flushed as he glanced at his father. "Yeah, I guess."

"What's your horse's name?" Margaret asked.

The boy's father, still leaning against the corral, answered, "Storm. He's twelve, a gelding, Percheron–Quarter Horse cross. Old enough to know better." He was coming toward her, his hands on slim hips molded into a pair of wranglers, and he was digging into each step with a dusty pair of boots. Margaret wanted to shrink back and find someplace to hide—maybe because she noticed he had arms a woman could get lost in. She figured he must have an arrogant attitude, too. The kid wasn't talking. It took Margaret a moment to realize how quickly he had shut down, instantly becoming a shadow behind his father.

"There are all kinds of horse people not more than twenty miles from here, around Spokane. They could do wonders, I'm sure," Margaret said. "What is it you think I can do for you?"

She didn't know why she was still talking. She wasn't qualified to do much of anything but lie out here and lick her wounds. It didn't help matters that she had also been falling on the wrong side of everything lately, including a three-hundred-year-old Kootenai County code. Living alone on a twenty-acre ranch in the entirely conservative northern Idaho panhandle wasn't entirely bad if you were a single man, but if you were a single woman, it just wasn't done. She knew that, and so did everyone else around here. What was wrong with this man? Didn't he know who she was?

"I'm not interested in taking my kid's horse to some yahoo in Washington State," he said. "Look, can you just take a look at the horse? That's all I'm asking."

The man was in her space now, right in front of her. Holy shit, was he tall. She was five foot nine, so he had to be at least six two, six three. She sidestepped away. Maybe he was one of those guys who got a kick out of tormenting women, because he stepped closer again, matching each step she took, like a slow dance, until she bumped the steps that led into the small house. She would have fallen flat on her backside if he hadn't reached out and grabbed her. He held her in a way that was familiar and close, stirring feelings in her that couldn't possibly be real. No, that was definitely not a road she would go down any time soon. She'd been there, done that, another reason she was hiding out here now.

"Kind of nervous, are you? Or is it me? Do you have a problem with me?" he said.

She couldn't look at him. Her face was burning, as she yanked herself away, pushing past him, fighting the urge to rub her arm where his hand had lingered almost possessively. She yanked the brim of her hat down and searched out the kid, who was pressed against the driver's door, hiding behind the rear-view mirror.

"I can't make any promises," she said, "but I'll take a look."

The man was standing right behind her. "Great. Can you come by today, say, this afternoon?"

No no no, she thought. She didn't want to go anywhere. She didn't want to leave this property today or any time soon. What had she gotten herself into? She couldn't do it, and she felt the icy fear paralyzing her like a surge of adrenaline until she glimpsed the boy. He searched her out with pleading eyes before jamming both hands in his baggy pants pockets and staring at the ground again. Margaret couldn't find her voice, so she nodded, swallowing a hard lump.

Mr. Good-looking stuck out his large, calloused hand.

"Great," he said. "I'm Joe Wilde. My son's Ryan. We're five miles up the road. I'll draw you a map."

Joe Wilde. Of course, she thought. He was one of the five Wilde boys she knew from childhood, all of whom had run the school and the county with their shenanigans. She had thought against hope that it might be him, the boy who'd haunted her childhood, teasing her mercilessly and christening her with a horrible nickname that had stuck with her until she moved away to attend medical school. The icy reality set in that unless he had suffered some sort of head injury, it would only be a matter of time before he realized who she really was. Then again, he only knew her as the "orange giant"—and every other crude version of the name that the kids had whispered in the sterile school halls. She doubted very much that he knew what her real name was.

Joe ripped an envelope in half from inside his truck and drew out a rough map. "Here, it's easy to find," he said. His fingers skimmed hers as he handed her the paper, invading her space again, standing right beside her. This time, he touched her shoulder as she struggled to decipher the pencilled lines and accompanying chicken scratch that would've made any doctor proud. She stiffened and smelled something pleasant before realizing it was him, not aftershave or cologne. She wondered how in the world soap and water could make a man smell that good. He might as well have been pressed right against her, as his heat was seeping into her as if they were two Eskimos pressed together under a bed of furs.... *Stop it!* she barked silently to stop her mind from going down that road.

She sidestepped again and dropped her hand, crumpling the paper. She went to step back but then tripped on his foot, dropping the mug. It shattered across the steps. He grabbed her and lifted her, knocking her hat off, and her mousy brown hair fell loose in disarray past her shoulders.

He set her down and then bent over to pick up her hat, brushing off the dust as he handed it to her. She snatched it away, stuck it on her head, and raced straight for the front door.

"So we'll see you this afternoon around two?" he shouted to her retreating back.

She didn't turn around as she stumbled up the two steps. "Yeah, uh-huh," she managed to mutter as she opened the door and slammed it behind her.

———

Joe stood outside the old log house with single-paned windows, the Spick house, watching the closed door Margaret Gordon had slammed in his face as if he were a leper and she couldn't get away from him fast enough. Just what the hell was the matter with the woman, anyhow?

She had always acted as though she had a stick shoved up her ass. All through school, she'd gone out of her way to avoid him, though she had mile-long legs that he had often pictured wrapped around him. Her long, thick, dark hair framed the most gorgeous smoky brown eyes and a cute round face. To top it off, she had a light smattering of freckles on her nose and cheeks that she never tried to hide with a pound of makeup. Her skin was flawless, and those lips—he dreamed of taking them for a test drive.

It was obvious the woman thought he was lower than a dung beetle. To tell the truth, he was embarrassed that his son had watched that woman try to emasculate him. Just what the hell was she doing, living out here all by herself, anyway? Last he heard, she'd hopped the first bus to Seattle for medical school. He'd seen her a few times over the years, and she had always had the same snobbish, stuck-up attitude, walking around as if she was better than everyone, looking right through him as if she didn't see him.

He'd seen her in town a few months back. She was tall and gorgeous, with a set of breasts he dreamed of running his hands over, feeling the weight of them. He had pictured what they'd look like, full and creamy with dark red nipples. Well, at the time, he'd nearly gone over and asked her out, but his common sense had kicked in, and he remembered that she had fought over money with her mother when her grandfather hadn't even been cold in the ground. Carl Spick would've rolled over in his grave if he'd seen the way his granddaughter and daughter acted, like two selfish moneygrubbers. Joe didn't need a woman like that in his life. Even now, he could barely make ends meet. With the economy in the toilet, he'd all but given up on ranching. He'd sold off the last of his cattle the year before Carl died and had started taking out trees here and there in the back, milling the lumber himself.

Here he was again, all because Stan Jerow had told him Margaret was still here. He had insisted that Margaret was who Joe needed for Ryan's horse, that she could work magic with any animal. Her grandfather had said Margaret had a special connection to them, a certain touch. Whatever was going on with his horse, Ryan's horse, Margaret would figure it out. When he'd driven in and seen her in that ratty old hat and wool coat, he'd felt poleaxed. He would never have believed a woman could make anything that frumpy look sexy. The way she had walked, all sexy in those faded blue jeans, along with the fact that she didn't need to curl and primp just to step outside, had all his good sense taking a hike, which was the one and only reason he had worked her until she agreed to come and see Storm. Whatever he was thinking with, it sure in the hell hadn't been his brain. As he bent over and picked up the broken mug, he reminded himself that he had until that afternoon to pull his head out of his ass, have her look at the horse and then send her on her way.

CHAPTER

Two

She'd changed three times, not that her small closet held many clothes. She didn't even have many outfits, since she had basically lived in scrubs during her residency. Since her encounter with Joe, she had shampooed and used the good conditioner on her hair in the small shower bath, and she'd spent the entire morning arguing with herself and racing around the small two-bedroom house. She'd also found the pieces of her pink and gold mug placed in a neat pile off to the side of the top step—and in a thoughtful way so she wouldn't cut herself.

It wasn't as if Joe Wilde had asked her out on a date, and this certainly wasn't a beauty pageant. She was going to see a dusty and dirty horse, and she'd be traipsing through horse shit. It wasn't lost on her that Joe Wilde hadn't changed one bit. He was still the same arrogant ass she'd gone to school with, always planning and scheming. He'd manipulated her into going over to see the damn horse, and in front of his kid, for God's sake! He was lower than a skunk. Deep down, she had silently, miserably suffered through her entire adolescence with a major crush on Joe and she was furious that he still had that effect on her.

After moving away, she'd been too busy with medical school to allow Joe to invade her every waking thought, and the crush had faded—sort of. When she returned after her grandfather died, she had seen him at the funeral. After all these years, she still recognized him. Even the devil himself would have had the decency to offer condolences, but not Joe. She had expected more from him, but he was still the same selfish jerk he'd been in school, leaving without saying one word. Even in town a few months back, she had pretended not to see him and hurried the other way, fearing the snake was just waiting to make a joke of her again. When he had driven up this morning with his kid and his devilish charm, she'd frozen.

Now, as she gazed in the mirror, about to apply a hint of makeup, reality hit her like a blast of frigid air. The man had a kid with him, his kid, so of course there had to be a wife. How pitiful. Drooling over a married man—how low had she sunk? To him, this was a game, and he was winding her around his finger. Why, she could just imagine the laugh he was having at her expense now. Joe Wilde: just the name said it all, just an average Joe, a redneck nobody from a small town in the backwoods USA. Hell, she was better than that. She had gone to medical school and worked herself to the bone, spending years surviving on catnaps and bad coffee, just to end up right back here.

She tossed her makeup back in the drawer and yanked a brush through the curls she'd spent the last hour styling into her hair. Short of washing it again, she didn't have a hope of getting rid of them, and she didn't have time to redo anything. She glanced at her small bedside clock and the rumpled unmade double bed covered with half the clothes in her closet. It was one forty-five, time to go.

Margaret stomped her feet into her comfortable square-toed boots, the old ones that were cracked and faded, and caught a glimpse in the hallway mirror of the pristine crispness of her freshly ironed white shirt and brand-new jeans. She didn't have time to change again, and the last thing she wanted was for Joe Wilde to think she'd dressed up and primped for him. The excuse that she had done it for the horse sure wouldn't fly, so she grabbed an old brown sweater and shrugged it on, slung her cloth purse over her shoulder, and set the wide-brimmed hat she always wore on her head before hurrying out the door.

Angel nickered, and Margaret called to her: "I'm sorry! I won't be long, and then I'll take you out." She rubbed the white star just above Angel's eyes and then peeked over the corral into the red plastic water tub, half full. She took off at a jog around the square house, which her grandfather had built for his bride from the trees on the property. After her residency, when she'd passed the boards, she had bought herself a used black Lexus that now sat in the back-yard. She had kept it even after returning to Post Falls, a town where all the residents drove pickups—another one of those damn codes she was breaking.

The five-mile drive to Joe's farm down the backcountry gravel road added a few more nicks to the midnight black of her sports car. The entire way, her foot trembled on the gas pedal as she argued with herself to turn around, go home and lock the door. She swore and told herself to suck it up and get the meeting over with. *Don't agree to anything he asks,* she warned herself.

She slowed and pressed the brake as she rounded a bend in a cloud of dust, stomping the clutch and throwing the gear into neutral when she saw the house number staked at the side of the tree-lined road. Tiny branches and early spring leaves hid a portion of the rotted sign, which seemed to have been painted in red by a two-year-old. The narrow driveway flanked by heavy brush resembled a mud bog similar to those from monster truck shows. She would need a four by four to get through, but where could she leave her car on this narrow gravel road, and how far up was the house? In this part of the country, people had large spreads and mile-long driveways, houses always hidden way out back.

She pressed her head back against the headrest. If she turned around and went home, Joe would just show up again and catch her off guard, and she didn't want that. No, she needed to get rid of him once and for all, set him straight. She didn't work with horses. She couldn't and wouldn't help him, and she planned to say just that, telling him to leave her the hell alone. Margaret stomped the clutch and backed up, the wheels scraping the gravel. She gave herself a quick pep talk, because she would need to get enough speed to sail through the mud. She was determined not to think of the worst-case scenario: If she took it slow and easy, she'd sink faster than a rock in water and would be spinning her wheels to the end of time. The thought of being stuck anywhere in Joe Wilde's clutches was enough of an incentive for her to rev the engine a couple of times, her foot hitting the accelerator as if she were at the starting line of the Kootenai County stock-car races, with testosterone pulsing all around her.

"Well, here goes," she muttered. She stomped the clutch, slipped the gear into second, and pressed the gas. The car jolted forward, the wheels grinding into the slick muck. It skidded sideways and, in a panic, Margaret cranked the wheel hard to the right and slid the other way. The radials spewed clumps of mud onto the windshield. Out of nowhere flashed a metal post, and she screamed, twisting the wheel, giving the car more gas. The car whipped around like a Tilt-A-Whirl, the front dipping down as the back end hit the post with the sound of grinding metal, jolting the car to a standstill. The shoulder strap dug into her shoulder, and Margaret gripped the leather steering wheel, sitting in a daze, her ears still ringing from the sharp sound of bent metal. The engine sputtered before her foot slipped off the clutch, and the car jerked forward and stalled.

"Well, that's just great." She yanked the handle and pushed open the door before thinking twice about stepping into the mud, which was now level with the floorboards. She crawled over the center console to the passenger side and slid down the window. The metal post was surrounded by the back panel of her car. Thick mud splattered the sides, and more paint had chipped away. She had almost made it another few feet to where the mud ended and the rest of the driveway began.

Margaret scooted back in her seat and slammed her door shut. She thought she could make it, so she cranked the engine and shifted into first, but the tires spun. She reversed and the same thing happened, the wheels spinning her sideways and deeper into the mud. Just the thought of being found here had her jamming the stick shift again into first, then second, giving it plenty of gas. Mud splattered her face and inside the car from the open passenger window, and she stopped again. "No!" she cried, taking in the mud everywhere, over the seat and the places on her white shirt where her brown sweater hung open.

"Hey, what the hell are you doing?" a man shouted.

Her driver's door was jerked open, and she glanced over all the mud and up into the questioning blue eyes of Joe Wilde. She didn't know how she did it, but her foot somehow slipped on the clutch, and the car jerked forward, knocking Joe on the shoulder. All six feet of solid muscle landed on top of her.

———

Joe couldn't believe what he'd found. He'd heard a car spinning its tires, and when he jumped into his big blue truck and stopped at the end of the driveway, he realized his mistake. He watched the black sports car spinning its wheels, the back end skidding from side to side, the driver crazed and wide eyed. What the hell was the matter with the woman? It was springtime, and the winter runoff created mud at every low point. His driveway, like most around here, wouldn't dry out until summer.

Her car had collided with the metal post and stalled. Joe thought she was absolutely nuts. He started to call out to her when she popped her head out the rolled-down passenger window, but she closed her door and started the car again. Mud flew everywhere, and he waved his arms but could do nothing but watch in horror as the car sank deeper and deeper into the sticky mud. She skidded and spun, and then she shrieked and the car stopped.

Joe raced over as quickly as he could in knee-high gumboots and slogged through the thick mud, yanking open her door. "Jesus, lady. What the hell are you doing?" he barked, staring in disbelief at the mud clumped and splattered everywhere on her face, her shirt and hair, and the interior of the car. She turned those cinnamon-brown eyes on him, seeming dazed and helpless before the car jerked forward, knocking him off balance. He landed on top of her, those lush, perfect breasts pressing into his chest. His groin tightened, and he wondered for a moment if she had planned that. His mind raced over how easy it would be to peel back her shirt and run his tongue over that lacy white bra and the creamy plumpness underneath, but she would probably scream and squeal—the prude—and worry that he was getting her dirty. Fat chance of that happening. He would only humiliate himself, so he yanked her keys from the ignition and moved off of her, his hand accidentally brushing her thigh.

When he leaned in this time, he was scowling.

———

Margaret was stunned, unable to comprehend how things had gone from bad to really stupid. She was sure he was about to tell her to take a hike. The way he glowered at her with those stormy blue eyes, she was sure she was the last person he'd let near his kid or horse. She was absolutely incompetent. Those were the exact words a father had screamed at her in the waiting area of Harborview Trauma Center after she'd botched what was supposed to have been a routine removal of a benign tumour on the temporal lobe of his seven-year-old boy, leaving him unable to communicate. Even worse, the boy could no longer recognize his father. The contempt showered on her by his parents had hollowed her to the point that she was filled with self-loathing.

"Are you okay?" Joe said. He clutched her keys, and she could feel a cold sweat bathing her face and back. He wiped her cheek and she flinched, and he pulled his fingers back as if he'd been burned. Squeezing his hand, he glared again as if he wanted to punch something. "Sorry, you've got mud on your face. Just what the hell are you doing, coming through here in a car? Everyone has a four by four in these parts. You don't live out here unless you do."

"Yeah, well, didn't have a chance to pick one up," she said. She glanced in the rear-view mirror, and horror filled her eyes. There was mud splattered on her face, in her hair. She wiped her cheek and then brushed away some of the clumps of mud dotting her white shirt, but she only managed to make it worse.

"Look, I'm going to have to tow you out of here. I've got a winch on my truck," he said, tapping the roof of her car as he leaned in. "Mud's deep. You got anything decent on your feet?"

"My riding boots," she replied, wiping her cheek one more time and sliding around to step out.

Joe scooped her up and lifted her in his arms. She shrieked, more out of shock and disbelief than anything else. No man had ever carried her, certainly not just to keep clumps of mud from her feet.

"For the love of God, woman, hang on," he barked out as he tossed her a bit to get a better grip.

She linked her arms around his neck, and the next thing she knew, he had yanked open the passenger door of his truck and dumped her on the seat.

"I'll come back and fish your car out. Ryan's waiting for you up by the house to show you his horse," he said, shoving her door closed. Margaret watched him through a dusty, grimy windshield as he walked around the front of the truck. His mood seemed dark as night. He didn't even glance her way when he knocked his big rubber boots against the side of the truck before sliding behind the wheel.

He started the truck and threw it in reverse, tossing his arm over the seat back and spinning the truck around so fast that she slid across the seat and bumped his arm. She grabbed the handle above the passenger door as his truck bounced over the ruts, which he didn't take slow and easy. Bouncing around, she silently kicked herself for not wearing her clunky sports bra instead of the silky thing that left nothing to the imagination. She tried to hang on and hold her sweater closed with her other hand, and she was so thankful to finally see the house, the barn and Ryan.

Ryan stood off to the side, near one of two square corrals. A pure black horse was alone in one, and the other held a palomino and a silver dapple. Joe braked sharply, and Margaret realized she would've landed on the floor if she hadn't been holding on. He jerked open his door and jumped out, slamming it so hard the truck shook. Margaret did a quick check: Her white shirt was ruined, and she'd only fastened two buttons on her sweater when her door was jerked open.

"You done powdering your nose, or are you coming?"

Boy, was Joe ever in a bad mood. Margaret realized she was batting zero with this guy. Why the hell had he shown up at her place to begin with? With the way he watched her, she wondered if he remembered what a hopelessly awkward misfit she had been all through school, never fitting in.

"You drive like an idiot," she blurted before sliding around. She went to step on the running board, but the mud coating it was slick, and her heel skidded. She would have tumbled face first in the dirt if Joe hadn't been there. Once again, she found herself in his arms, nose to nose this time, so close he could have leaned in and kissed her with those firm red lips. She had no doubt he knew how to kiss a woman properly and thoroughly and that he had plenty of practice. Any focus she had completely scattered as her face heated, because for one awkward, delirious moment, she thought he was going to kiss her. She wished he'd lean in and press his lips to hers, but instead he loosened his arms enough that she slid down, feeling every hard male part of him, before he released her and stepped back.

He cleared his throat. "Ryan, get over here," he said. Even in her rattled haze, she didn't miss the sharpness in his tone. Yup, he was pissed, all right. She crossed her arms, because so was she.

Ryan walked over in the most unhurried, aggravating way, dragging his heels, slouching his shoulders in an old jean jacket. His long hair covered his eyes, but his behavior let his dad know how miserably unhappy he was about doing anything he was asked.

"Which one's your horse?" Margaret said, using the moment to stifle the tension that had erupted between father and son. She was sure Joe had been about to plant his foot in Ryan's backside, something her own grandfather had done to counter her smart-mouthed teenage attitude.

"The black one, alone in the corral. We can't put any horses in with him because he'll kick them," Joe barked. "Don't either of you set a foot in there until I get back."

Margaret watched the range of emotions on Joe's face —frustration, irritation—unsure whether they were for her or Ryan. Then he was gone in his truck, spinning around, the engine roaring, dust and gravel following him back down that long, rutty driveway.

When she glanced at Ryan, she saw he stood a little straighter and brushed his hair from his forehead as if an invisible weight had been lifted from him. Then again, she had breathed a little easier, too, but for a different reason. Margaret glanced back at the trail where the truck had disappeared and took a minute to do the one thing she was good at, listening and paying attention to what wasn't being said, particularly between father and son.

"He's beautiful. How long have you had him?" Margaret asked. She strode to the corral and leaned against the rough bark post, watching the horse on the far side. The corral was dirt with thick mud at one end where it sloped down, uneven, holding a wood hay trough and a blue plastic water barrel.

She didn't look directly at Ryan but caught the sharp shrug of his shoulders. Margaret waited until he stepped closer again, his hands still deep in his pockets.

"Dad got him for me the year after Mom died."

His mother had died? Her heart broke for him, and she swallowed her unshed tears. "How long ago did she die?" she asked, watching the horse head to the fence on the other side of the corral. It refused to give any attention to Ryan, its ear twisting to her when she spoke and then away.

"I was five when she died. I hardly remember her now."

"Your dad never remarried?" she said. She couldn't believe she had asked him that, and she suddenly wished to take it back. "I mean…"

"No," he snapped.

She needed to change the subject fast, but she was torn between her sorrow for the grieving boy and her frustration at the spark of joy she had felt at hearing Joe was single. What was wrong with her? She wanted to kick herself hard, because any fantasy about her and Joe would only get her heartbroken and humiliated again. "How old are you?"

"Fourteen. Well, almost. My birthday's coming up." He was now right beside her, staring at the horse and glancing awkwardly at her.

"When's your birthday?"

"Next week," he said.

She did the quick math: Joe was her age, thirty-two, so he had to have been eighteen when Ryan was born. Margaret had graduated early, and she didn't remember who he had been seeing, but he'd always had some spunky good-looking girl hanging off his arm. Margaret had left Post Falls right after that, and she hadn't followed any of the gossip, not that her grandfather had tried to keep her abreast of the happenings in town.

Ryan was about as talkative as she was, and Margaret had gone weeks without human contact or conversation with anything other than her horse. She was terrible at small talk, and obviously, so was Ryan, so the awkwardness lingered.

"So, tell me about your horse and what's going on," she said. She brushed away some dried mud from a spot on her forehead that had begun to itch.

"He steps on my foot if I try to get a halter on him. He's charged me, tried to bite me, bumped into me. I can't get a bridle on him. He tosses his head every time I try. If I manage to get the halter on and over his ears, I can't get the bit in his mouth. He won't open it, and I'm afraid he'll bite me."

"When was the last time you rode him?" Margaret asked. She could see there was nothing easy about this horse.

"The last time I tried to get on him was about a month ago, and he threw me. I never saw it coming. He was tossing his head back and forth, wiggling around and the next thing I knew, I had landed on the ground. Dad saddled him then for me. He fought Dad, too," Ryan said.

"Does your dad know you're scared of him?" Margaret was starting to get the impression that Joe was more about forcing the kid, possibly overpowering the horse and showing him who was boss, a typical redneck attitude. It really didn't surprise her.

She could hear Joe's truck approaching. Ryan stepped away from the corral, his shoulders slumped. The sulky kid with a chip on his shoulder had returned. Margaret deliberately kept her back to Joe, but she could hear the slam of the truck door and sensed him approaching.

"I hauled your car out and parked it on the side of the road. Here're your keys," he said, dangling them just above her open palm and dropping them only when she looked up. "There's a nice dent in the back panel where you connected with the post, too. If you're going to be staying in these parts, get yourself a decent truck. So what have you two been talking about?" He glanced at Ryan before staring at Margaret with a look that said she better not be messing with his son.

Margaret could feel how tightly wound Ryan was beside her, worried she'd bring up his fear. There was an obvious disconnect between the two, secrets aplenty between father and son. Combined with the distrust between her and Joe, it made for an untidy mess. Margaret opened her mouth to say something, then closed it and smiled nervously as those damn butterflies fluttered inside her stomach. Just standing so close to the man had an effect on her, as if she had a hope in hell of pursuing him. *Don't go there. Think of something else,* she told herself. She finally stared at the horse, who had given all of them his backside. "Have you ridden this horse, Joe?" she asked. "Can you get near him?"

Joe moved right beside her, leaning his arms over the post, so close that she wished he'd take that half step more to touch her. *Don't look at him. Look somewhere else.*

"A few times. He's got a hard, squirrelly attitude. He's not easy to saddle, but I manage to get it on him. He's gotten worse this year. That horse has a serious attitude problem."

Margaret had never considered herself an expert with horses. She just understood them better than people.

People weren't honest—horses were. That summed it up perfectly.

"Ryan, go grab Storm's halter. Get it on him," Joe said.

"Joe, I don't think that's necessary," Margaret began, but Joe interrupted her.

"No, I want you to see the problems with this horse." He gestured sharply toward a small shed. "Ryan, get moving."

The boy jumped and hurried to the shed, returning with a green halter and a frayed lead rope knotted here and there, similar to her own tack. Margaret watched the boy hesitate at the gate, lift the looped rope over the nail that served as the latch, and slip inside the corral. Margaret stepped around Joe to the gate.

"Stay to the side. Keep away from his back end. Are you sure you want to do this?" she whispered to Ryan as she took the rope latch.

His face was pink, and his dark blue eyes widened with a deep terror she'd seen before. Fear wasn't good around any animal, let alone a twelve-hundred-pound horse that fed off every one of his feelings. She could see how this was about to go from bad to worse.

"Get the halter on. What are you waiting for?" Joe shouted as he moved behind Margaret. The man wasn't about to give his kid a break and she honestly worried he was about to get Ryan killed.

"Joe, seriously—stop," Margaret said, knowing she sounded worried.

Ryan had taken no more than two steps when Storm bolted the other way, rearing up and charging him, then bucked in a circle not more than a foot from Ryan's head. To the kid's credit, he was quick. He dropped the halter and leaped up and over the rail just as the horse tried to bite him.

"Ryan!" Margaret shouted and ran toward him.

Ryan's face was pasty white as he sat on the ground, breathing as if he'd run a marathon.

"Are you okay? Did he hurt you?" She crouched down and touched his arm.

Ryan stared into the dirt as he slowly shook his head.

"Damn horse. Told you he was crazy," Joe barked out.

"Crazy? You're crazy, making your kid go in there when he's not ready!" she snapped. "He didn't even know what to do, and that horse is a herd animal, looking for leadership, clearly knowing he won't get it from Ryan." She fisted her hands, and she wanted to knock Joe's teeth out. "That horse was feeding off fear and your bullying attitude. Ryan isn't ready to go in there. You're going to get your son killed if you insist on sending him into a situation he's not prepared for." She was in his face, shouting.

"Prepared? What the hell, lady? He's grown up in these parts. He's not some numbskull kid with no good sense. It's that damn horse! You just saw what that horse did. I need to get my gun and put it down!" Joe shouted back, his nose inches from hers. His warm breath had that same minty smell with a hint of coffee: pleasant, good. He stepped toward her, and she wondered for a minute if he was about to shake her. She stepped back, realizing her mistake. This man wasn't some brainy intern she could shout at and expect to simply take it.

She faced him with her arms crossed. "What I saw was a horse reacting to a bad situation," she said. "There are only two things a horse knows, being a prey animal. Horses are first cautious, then curious. You have no authority over Storm. He's made that clear. You have to earn his respect."

"Really? I suppose you think you can change that," Joe said, taking another step into her space. He was tall, and she was eye to eye with his chin. She wanted to thump his chest but thought better of it. After all, she wanted to get away from him as quickly as possible. She told herself that, but the problem was that every other part of her thought differently. Damn her traitorous body!

"I can do a hell of a lot better than that," she barked at him, not stepping back this time when he leaned closer, her heart pounding. The bottom of her stomach fell out when she realized what a stupid thing she had just done.

Joe smiled.

Margaret hadn't slept well. The sun was already up, shining through the tiny window, by the time she rolled out of bed. Her small, boxlike room was the only bedroom in the house with furniture, as she had hauled her grandfather's worn-out junk to the dump. Her room still held her childhood furniture, the same white dresser, nightstand, and matching headboard with flowers carved into the wood. It was a girl's bedroom, one she'd grown up in.

She stumbled barefoot on the icy wood floor, completely out of sorts, all because she'd been outsmarted by a man—well, not just any man: Joe Wilde. She had realized too late that he'd controlled their entire argument yesterday, if not the whole situation. He was an absolute master at directing behavior, mainly hers, and she'd walked right into it. She had no intention of working with that horse, or so she tried to tell herself, but now she remembered what a clever kid Joe had been at school. He could talk his way into or out of any situation he wanted, always in a way that made other people think it was their idea. As with most things, he'd gotten better with age. Crap!

Storm was to be sent to her by trailer this morning so she could spend time getting to know him and getting to the bottom of his issues. She already suspected his issues were rooted in the problems between Ryan and Joe, which neither was too willing to share, at least not with her. Yeah, something was going on, all right. Finding out now that Ryan's mom had died and Joe was still single brought a whole slew of questions and scenarios to mind, which irritated the hell out of her, since Joe was solely responsible for her restless night.

He'd all but invaded every one of her dreams, teasing her with kisses, and she swore she could feel his large, calloused hands skimming over her backside. She wondered what it would be like to have a man like that sharing her bed, her life, her…And then, of course, that made her angry, and she punched her pillow, because the idea of Joe Wilde having any interest in "Margaret the Misfit" was a fantasy her overworked, lonely brain had obviously conjured up.

The fact of the matter was that Margaret's life was a disaster. So what was she doing, pretending to be some professional trainer? Hadn't she made it clear to Joe that she didn't work with horses? She felt like a fake, a fraud, taking on a problem horse as if she had the skill and experience, as if she was a damn horse whisperer. She definitely wasn't that. Those were all big macho men who camped out in the fields, spending their time with horses and no one else. *Hang on a second,* she thought, because that was exactly what she'd been doing for the past six months with Angel. That was different, though. Angel was her friend, her companion and the only thing that gave her any peace. Angel was kind and soft and responsive to her. The horse always knew what Margaret was thinking before she did.

Margaret threw on a pair of old jeans and a plain t-shirt and stepped into deep rubber boots, jamming a ratty wide-brimmed hat on her head before stepping outside with her morning coffee. She pulled up the collar of the old coat she wore, and this time, as she stood in front of the old house, facing the acres of forested land, the sunlight brightened and flickered over the white markers of the family graveyard in the clearing. It had been bordered with a waist-high picket fence at the edge of the trees. Margaret found herself walking over to it and taking in the graves of the grandmother she'd never met and the three babies who had been stillborn, leaving her mother an only child. The newer grave of her grandfather still hadn't settled and still bore a rounded mound of dirt.

Margaret glanced up and took a breath. She supposed her grandfather had known that her mother had no interest in an eighty-acre backwater spread in northern Idaho, because he'd left everything to Margaret, including a mountain of debt, a hundred cows and a house so old that she swore the wiring had to be from the turn of the century. In between her residency at a Seattle hospital and driving back to Post Falls every week, she'd sold the cattle, found homes for her grandfather's horses and emptied the house. But something had stopped her just short of sticking a for-sale sign on the property and walking away. Maybe it was the fact that her grandfather hadn't given up on her, despite his quiet surliness and hardass ways. She knew deep down he loved her, and not once had he left her, even though everything and everyone irritated the hell out of him.

She was about to lean down and yank the weeds up from the grave when she heard a vehicle coming down the driveway. It wasn't just any vehicle. She would have known the especially loud vibrating purr of that four by four chewing up her ground anywhere. It was Joe's truck. The bottom of her stomach dropped out again. "Well, crap," she muttered. She raced to the house, spurred by every one of her pathetic insecurities, instead of standing there like a ninny, as she had the day before. The door banged the side of the house as she flew through it, dropping her coffee mug on the table, kicking off her boots, tossing her hat and coat on the floor. She raced down the narrow hall into the bathroom, quickly brushed her teeth, and ran a brush through her sleep-tousled hair. *Hurry up!* she told herself as the toothpaste suds dripped from her mouth. She dunked her head under the tap to rinse her mouth and quickly splashed water on her face, grabbing the towel and wiping it just as she heard the horn blast. Her heart was racing as she glanced in the mirror at her wrinkled shirt. She sniffed her pits, nearly gagged and she grabbed the deodorant. A quick swipe under her shirt was the best she could do. She jammed her feet into the rubber boots, grabbing her jean jacket off the hook and pulling it on as she raced out the front door. She skidded to a stop as the excitement and anticipation of seeing Joe fled.

Joe Wilde was leading Storm from a rusty horse trailer, and Ryan stood awkwardly in front of the truck and waved to her before jamming both hands in his baggy jean pockets—but that wasn't what set her teeth on edge. A gorgeous blonde slipped out of the driver's side. She wore tan capris and a matching jacket, and she was cute, with long, wavy hair and curves in all the right places. She waved at Margaret as if they'd known each other their whole lives.

"Oh, you must be Madeline. Joe was just raving last night about how good you are with horses. He says you're going to get Ryan's horse all calm and fixed up and take care of everything so that Ryan can ride him."

"Margaret," Ryan muttered.

"Pardon?" The blonde, who was petite too, paused and stared at Ryan.

"Her name's Margaret Gordon," Ryan said again.

Margaret could do nothing but stand there, just as she had done in school when Joe yanked off her wool cap the morning she'd tried to dye her hair blond but turned it orange instead. Everyone had roared with laughter, and she had been made the butt of a big joke. Why she remembered that horrific memory now was beyond her, except maybe she felt the same way. Even though no one was laughing at her, she felt as though she'd been kicked in the gut, the rug yanked out from under her. She'd misread something somewhere, so really, her anger was misplaced. It had to be, she tried to tell herself, but right about now, what she pictured was planting her foot right between Joe's legs and watching him fall over and cry.

"Oh, I'm sorry," the blonde said. "Well, Margaret, Madeline, the names are so close!" She actually waved her hand in front of her face and giggled, a squeaky, pathetic sound that had Margaret wanting to slap her.

The woman froze and pressed her hand against her chest, her eyes widening. Maybe the hostility Margaret was feeling actually showed on her face. She glanced at the worried look on Ryan's face and she smiled, or tried to, but it was downright impossible when inside, she felt like a love-starved idiot. For the life of her, she couldn't manage to say anything.

"Morning," Joe said. "Hope we're not too early." His hair was neatly combed, and his plaid shirt looked freshly ironed. He walked over and placed his arm around the blonde's shoulder, as she leaned into him, her head not topping his shoulder as she placed a hand with bright pink fingernails flat on his chest and fluttered her eyelashes up at him.

Joe smiled down at the blonde in a way that left Margaret feeling empty and pathetic. For a minute, in her rattled brain, she wondered if she had actually flinched. Her face ached, forcing a hard smile to her lips, and she wanted nothing more than to slink back inside and hide. It was only the thought of Ryan, who stood lost and alone in front of Joe's truck, looking like an outsider, mirroring exactly how she felt, that kept her there.

"This is Sara." Joe squeezed the blonde's shoulder, pressing her tighter against his side. There was no mistaking how involved they were.

"Hi," Margaret said. That was it, the sum of anything intelligent she could utter. She fisted her hands in awkwardness and then jammed them in her back pockets, trying to figure out what she could say and what the hell to do with her hands.

"Storm's all yours," Joe said. "Tied him to your corral, there. Didn't think you'd want him in with your horse." He inclined his head to where the horse was tied. Well, of course he couldn't use his hand, because it was glued to the skinny tart plastered against him. Margaret could only stare. Joe cleared his throat. "You okay?"

Her face heated, and that prompted her forward. "Hi, Ryan," she said. She kept going, because her insides were jittery and her face, she knew, was now bright red. Storm must have picked up on her anxiety, because he started fidgeting and stepping sideways. "You know, it might be best if I get him settled now. You can go," she said. She didn't turn around but shut her eyes, counting back from ten and then taking a deep breath. She needed them gone before she jammed her other foot in her mouth, but when she turned around, three sets of eyes stared back and she had a sinking feeling they thought she'd lost her mind.

"Uh, you sure you're okay with him?" Joe asked, gazing down at the blonde and then back at her.

She noted how different his demeanor was from the day before. He wasn't barking, shouting or being an ass, period. His peacock feathers were in full bloom. She pressed her lips together harder and went to yank the brim of her hat down, except her finger came up empty, grabbing nothing but air. The damn hat was on the floor inside, so she awkwardly slapped her head. "Yeah, uh-huh."

"Well, okay then." Joe laughed in a happy, lighthearted way that made her heart sink even more. He placed his hand on Sara's back, pulled open the driver's door, and helped her in—with his hand on her ass, no doubt.

Ryan still had his hands stuffed in his pockets, standing awkwardly, another outsider just like her. She sympathized.

"So you'll call me after and let me know what's happening, and make sure you stay safe with that horse?" Joe said, jabbing a finger at her. She stared at him, wondering who this guy was and feeling tempted to give him the finger.

Ryan climbed in the passenger side. Margaret stepped back, and Joe started the truck and turned in a wide circle, the horse trailer rattling from where it was hitched behind the truck. Joe honked and waved as he drove past, smiling and laughing with Sara pressed against his side and Ryan looking the other way.

Margaret waited until the taillights disappeared, taking the happy couple with them, and she wondered where her head was. Somehow in all this, she'd unconsciously shoved her and Joe into some happy bubble, which had burst and dumped her right on her ass in the gutter.

"Stupid, stupid," she said. "First the man tricks you into looking after his fricking horse, and where in the hell did you get the idea a guy like him could be single? Joe

Wilde," she barked at herself. Storm blew out his nostrils to let her know he was still there. "Okay, where to put you?" She glanced at Angel, her Arabian mare, who hung her head over the corral.

"You're going into the field, my girl," Margaret said as she grabbed Angel's halter, unlatched the gate and led her out, but not before she stopped and stared at the prickly dark horse, the reason her self-imposed isolation had ended in the most unexpected and uneasy way.

"You told me she was the next best thing to Monty Roberts in this part of the panhandle. That she's got a gentle touch and can straighten out Storm, find out what the horse's problem is, but the only thing I'm seeing is an uptight broad with a pole shoved too far up her ass. She hasn't changed one bit from school," Joe said as he slammed his fist on the pressboard counter at the feed store.

Stan Jerow and his wife, Hazel, were the hub of Post Falls. Well into their seventies, they knew everything about everyone. Stan had been close friends with Carl Spick, Margaret's crotchety old grandfather. He frowned from behind his bifocals. "Now, I think you're misreading things a bit there. She's a hardnose, but Margaret's got a heart of gold."

"Yeah, gold, my ass. More like gold-digger," Joe barked. "I've got a mind to go back over there and pick Storm up. Last thing I need is him hurting her. She'd be coming after me next, suing me for everything."

"You know Margaret's not like that," Stan said. "She's

a good girl. Had a hard time, you know, growing up. Just give her a chance." He called out to the back room, "Hazel, Joe's here about the Gordon girl!"

Hazel Jerow was the other half of the husband–wife team that ran the feed store, and she could talk anyone's ear off for an hour, catching up on all the community gossip. She always had big curls from the rollers that she was sure to set in her thin gray hair every night.

"Now, Joe, don't you go fretting about Margaret," Hazel said, tapping his arm with her bony, wrinkled hand. "She's a tough girl. I've seen her take her own mama down a peg or two, and that woman has ice water flowing through her veins. If you'd seen her with Angel, what she got her to do, why, that horse follows her around like a puppy dog now." She patted his hand this time. "Remember, Stan? Every time we go out there, she's with that horse, talking away to it. With the way that horse responds to her, well, let's say she's got the touch."

"Touch, my ass," Joe scoffed. "All I've seen is a woman who annoys the hell out of me, and that's when she's not tripping all over herself to run the other way."

Stan and Hazel exchanged a glance. "Hmm," Stan said, and Hazel clucked her tongue. Then they both smiled in the way people do when they know something you don't.

"What?" Joe asked, stifling the urge to slam his fist on the counter.

They exchanged a look again, and it was Hazel who spoke. "Well, you make the girl nervous, always have, and she's having a rough time after what happened to that little boy."

"What little boy? What are you talking about?" Joe asked again.

"The reason she's home, some boy she was operating

on. All I know is what she told me. She made a mistake on a simple surgery, a simple tumor, she said, and something went wrong. The kid couldn't talk or recognize his parents. She'd left him brain damaged," Hazel whispered loudly.

Joe had known Margaret was some highfalutin' surgeon, but he didn't know why she was back in Post Falls. "I just thought she was back here, getting the place ready to sell," he said.

Joe remembered when old Carl Spick had died alone. He had gotten a frantic call from Stan Jerow about how Hazel had found the crotchety old guy's decomposing body. He'd driven as if the hounds of hell were on his heels down to the Spick house, beating the emergency services, and he'd stood in the background and listened when Hazel called Margaret and told her the news. He'd even rode out on his horse when Stan Jerow asked him to and found the one hundred or so cows Carl owned. Although they were fine, with plenty of pasture to graze and a large pond to keep them watered, he rounded them up and brought them in so Stan could look after them until something else could be figured out.

He worried about Margaret and had even come to pay his respects, offering his help. But the day of the funeral, Margaret's high-class corporate mother had shown up at the farm in a chauffeured limousine, stirring up all kinds of shit, and he'd overheard them arguing about selling the place and money and who got what. Well, he'd walked the other way. He never thought Margaret would be a money-grubbing high-society snob like her mother. Joe couldn't believe it.

"Sell? Hell, no," Stan said, almost choking, and Hazel stared at Joe as if he had a screw loose. "She'd never sell the Spick place. She promised her grandfather. My God,

Carl and Mary and their three young 'uns are buried there. That just wouldn't be right."

"Well, then, why is she still here?"

They stared at each other again, and Stan cleared his throat. "She was fired," he said.

The day had warmed up quite nicely. Margaret had spent two hours working Storm in the round ring, and she was breathing as hard as the horse, but by God she felt good—no, great. The first day, she had spent time watching Storm, figuring out who he was. He had a strong mind and energy, not an easy horse for someone young and green, with no self-confidence, and definitely not a horse for some cowboy who thought to control him, because that wasn't going to happen. No, the first day for Margaret was all about small steps, and she took all of them. The second day had been better, although Storm made nothing easy. She worked hard, keeping her circle out, not letting her energy wane. Oh, he challenged her, bucking, changing directions, leaping around, showing her how strong minded he was.

This wasn't about overpowering him, because overpowering a twelve-hundred-pound animal wasn't even logical. This was all about gaining trust, getting him to recognize that whatever problems or distractions were going on out there, she would protect him. Only then was change going to happen. And only through her calm, steady approach. Only one of two things happened in a ring: Either the rider took on the erratic, high-strung behavior of the horse, or the horse would eventually calm to the powerful energy of the rider. It was about who was stronger, as well as hard work. Staying focused, balanced and well away from Storm's hooves was a challenge, Margaret had to admit. A challenge she was enjoying every minute of, because it took her mind from her problems, from going to that dark, lonely place where she'd lived in silence for the past six months.

On the second day, when she was covered in sweat and her thin t-shirt felt glued to her back, and every inch of her was covered in dust and grime from head to toe, and she swore her teeth were filled with so much grit that she'd be eating it for dinner, Storm turned and faced her, licking his lips. She took that one tiny gesture. Because, for Storm, it was a huge step toward trust. The third day was when magic truly happened. When she tossed hay into the trough for Angel and then into the round ring where she kept Storm, he stepped forward calmly, his head down, and the dynamic presence that he scared everyone with was dimmed. "Good boy," she said, patting his side, and he let her. She quietly left him to eat, taking that huge victory with her, knowing when to quit and walk away.

Margaret had just cleaned up the corral and was pushing a wheelbarrow of manure around the side of the shed when she heard the unmistakable purr of Joe's monster truck. Her tan t-shirt was coated in grime, her hair pulled back in a ponytail. When the dark blue truck appeared, it sent her heart skittering again. Instead of being neighborly and friendly, she scowled as Joe slid out. She looked this time but didn't see a blonde, and she let out a sigh of relief. Ryan climbed out of the passenger side, and Storm, who was in the riding ring, started whinnying and stomping his hooves, snorting. The whites of his eyes flared with an attitude she hadn't seen during the time he had been with her.

"Hadn't heard from you. I thought you were going to call," Joe said. He slammed his door and walked straight to her in his sexy, he-man way. All she could see was how he was with Sara, and it hurt.

"I don't have a phone," she said.

He stopped as if she'd tossed a pail of ice water on him. "You don't have a phone, seriously?" he said, scratching his head.

Margaret shrugged. "Hey, Ryan," she said before lifting the wheelbarrow and continuing away from them toward the manure pile around the side of the corral, closer to the line of trees. She dumped it and looked up at Joe, who was following her with a puzzled look.

"Why didn't you tell me you didn't have a phone when I brought Storm over?" he said. "I asked you…"

"No, you told me to call you. I recall I didn't answer," she said, cutting him off. She lifted the handles of the wheelbarrow and turned to walk away, but Joe grabbed her arm just above the elbow.

"Is there a problem?" he said. Margaret stared at the warm, rough hand that held her, and he dropped it. "Look, we just came to find out how it's going with Storm. Maybe this is a waste of time.…"

"Storm has done very well," she said, gesturing to him and noticing his skittish behavior. "This is the first time he's reacted this way since being here. We're working on trust, building it slowly between us. This is a step back, what I'm seeing here." She moved away from Joe.

"Well, that's great. Could we see what you're doing?"

There weren't very many rules Margaret lived by, but

having anyone watch her, judging the few capabilities she had, wasn't going to happen, not here, and definitely not with Joe. "I'm not comfortable with that yet. I work alone. I'm building trust with Storm, and I can't do that with someone watching over me. For one, look at how he's reacting now with you two here." Margaret glanced at Ryan, who was standing in the grassy field between the corral and round ring, watching Storm. "Would you mind if Ryan stayed?"

Joe crossed his arms. "I suppose that would be okay. You have something in mind?"

"Joe, can I ask you something?" she said. She took in his unshaven face and large nose, which made him look entirely too dangerous to her, even though she had pined for him as a kid. She glanced at his shoulders, which were wide and solid like a quarterback's, and then finally turned her back on him completely.

"What are you doing?" He actually started laughing at her, stepping in front of her and resting both hands on her shoulders. "I can't talk to you if you're going to keep turning your back on me or running the other way. Stand still, will you?"

"I'm sorry I can't look at you…. I mean, I'm not used to having people around." This really wasn't going well, and she considered sticking her head in a hole and hiding.

"I'm not going to bite," he said. "Unless you ask really nicely, that is."

Her face burned, and she gaped at the devil who grinned before her. She brushed his arm away and shut her eyes, he was laughing at her again.

"You're a nervous thing, aren't you?" he said.

"What…? No! Listen, you're distracting me. I wanted to ask you about Ryan. Did something happen recently between him and Storm? I mean, from what I understand, you've had Storm for what, ten years? This is a recent problem that's come up, so it makes me think something happened. This isn't about people with horse problems, it's about a horse with people problems. Horses only feel guarded if there's a reason." She didn't want to say that horses reacted to the pressure of people's elevated emotional energy. She sensed that a problem had been building and building for a long time. Until she got to the root of what that problem was, she had no hope of connecting Ryan with his horse.

Joe appeared to consider what she said, then gave a dismissive wave, as if she didn't know what she was talking about. "I think you're reading too much into it. I'll leave Ryan and be back later for him, since you don't have a phone," he said before turning toward the corral and calling out to his son. "Ryan, I'm you leaving you here! I'll come back later to pick you up."

He left without another word to Margaret, and judging by his sharp reaction, she wondered if she'd hit a very sensitive nerve.

"Please come to my birthday party! I really want you there," Ryan asked with bright, innocent eyes—eyes far different from the morose ones he saved exclusively for his dad. Margaret hadn't seen Joe since the day he left Ryan and came back three hours later, honking his horn and driving away without even a wave for Margaret. That had been three days ago.

"Ryan, I can't. I don't do so well around people. I'm just not comfortable. Besides, your dad's giving you this party. I don't think he'd want me there." Margaret hung up Storm's halter and left him in the large, fenced-off field to graze with Angel, who was calm and balancing against Storm's fiery personality. Margaret rested her forearms on top of the fence.

"Please, Margaret? I don't have very many friends, and I really want you there. Besides, you're wrong—Dad does like you." Ryan was squirming beside her, shuffling from one booted foot to the other. She didn't miss the hopeful look on his face.

"You didn't tell me your dad had a girlfriend. Sara, is

it?" she asked. She knew darn well it was, as the woman's name was burned into her brain. Spending time, even five minutes at Ryan's birthday, watching Sara and Joe fall all over each other like two love-starved puppies, was about as appealing as a root canal.

"I wouldn't exactly say she's Dad's girlfriend," Ryan replied.

Well, that got her attention. She scratched her elbow and watched something in the boy's eyes that had her backing up. "Oh no, you're not trying to matchmake, are you, set me up with your dad?"

"You two would be great together!" he said. "Look how you've helped Storm! He's so calm with you, and Dad listens to you."

"No, he doesn't. Your dad doesn't like me. He never did," she barked, shocked at what Ryan had said even though she silently wished for just that. She would die before ever admitting it to herself, let alone telling anyone. "Why, Ryan? What's wrong with Sara? I mean, your dad looked really happy with her," she said. As she spoke, she saw the loss and disappointment in Ryan and started to connect some things, like a roadmap of secrets, and Storm was the key. "How long has your dad been dating Sara?"

"About a month, I guess. Not long. He had a couple girlfriends at one time."

Margaret pushed away from the corral and stared at the scraped blue mountain bike Ryan had rode over on. She'd dealt with this kind of stuff in her residency, having to mask her judgment during difficult conversations. She must have been slipping, because right now she wanted nothing more than to go over and kick Joe somewhere that'd make him think twice about engaging in such things. She loathed guys like that.

"So your dad dated two women at once. That must have been awkward for you."

Ryan actually smirked. "Only when I slipped up and called one the wrong name. Dad gave me one of those looks that let me know I was in big trouble, but she knew. I think it was Patti, or maybe it was Peggy. Can't remember —there've been so many. Dad never saw her again."

"You did that deliberately, didn't you?" she said.

He shrugged, and she noticed the sadness return.

"How many women have there been?" She tried to keep her voice light, but what she was hearing gave her a whole different view of Joe, and not in a good way.

"I don't know, really. I lost count. After Dad got his computer, he signed up for online dating about three years ago. I'd see him on the computer after dinner at night, chatting with women. He'd meet them for coffee, have them out for dinner, even took me with him a few times into town. There was one named Julie—I liked her, but she was last year, a schoolteacher and a good cook, too. She was pretty, like you, but Dad got this weird look in his eye after she spent the night one time, and I knew she wouldn't be back," Ryan replied with a forlorn look.

Margaret wondered what kind of stupid expression was on her face, because she couldn't believe Ryan had called her pretty. She had to blink a couple times and swallow. Margaret had never been pretty. She'd been awkward, too tall as a teen, but she'd never once considered herself pretty. She cleared her throat. "Why don't you like Sara?"

He gave her a look as if she had sprouted a second head. "She's not real! Everything is fake about her, and I don't think she tells the truth. I know she doesn't like me, though. She pretends with Dad, always hanging on his arm, completely useless. She'd never do what you do, scoop up manure. She hates the dirt, and when we were at her place in town, she shrieked when I almost sat on her white couch."

Margaret smiled. "Were your pants dirty?" She laughed and couldn't shake that picture from her head.

"I don't know. I didn't check, but Dad got after me. She stays over sometimes and makes a lot of noise in Dad's room, carrying on. She giggles a lot. It's annoying."

Margaret watched the hopeful look on Ryan's face and gazed out at the peaceful sight of Storm munching happily with Angel. "Okay, I'll come," she said.

"You will, really? You won't regret it. It's going to be a great party now." Ryan threw his arms around her neck and hugged her, then bounced up and down.

Margaret then realized the enormity of what she'd just agreed to. Panic, dread, and every fear imaginable had her breaking out in a cold sweat, but she saw the hopeful look on Ryan's face, and she knew she couldn't let him down.

What do you get a fourteen-year-old boy? Margaret asked herself. She certainly hadn't considered all the ramifications of her decision to go to Ryan's party. First she had to drive to town, which she had avoided since returning. Although Post Falls was large enough, the chances of running into anyone she might recognize were high, and she worried the entire way into town to the hardware store, her foot shaking on the gas pedal. She eventually spied a great pocket knife that had tons of gadgets and hoped Ryan didn't already have one.

She recognized the redheaded balding guy behind the counter from school. It was Rick, one of Joe's old friends. He'd stared at her when she asked to see the knife, and he had even asked her name, but thankfully, when she told him, it hadn't seemed to register. By the time she got home, she didn't have much time to get ready, as the barbeque started at five. She hadn't done any work at all that day with Storm because she'd been worrying about the party. And what did one wear to a party for a fourteen-year-old, anyway? She wasn't going to know anyone there—well, except Ryan, Joe and that blond bimbo who would be hanging off his arm.

She settled on a nice pair of blue jeans and a green shirt, but nothing would dim her debilitating fear of going over to Joe's. She didn't know who was going to be there. Would there be kids, adults and how many? She wondered how painful the night would be, and the more she thought about it, the more she was sweating.

She drove her car, but this time she pulled close to the shoulder and left it parked on the side of the road. There was a path beside the entrance that wasn't as muddy, and she made her way up the driveway—a walk that didn't take as long as she hoped. She could hear voices and laughter, a definite party atmosphere. She walked into the open, grassy yard, where a picnic table and several plastic chairs were sitting, and about a dozen adults and that many more kids all stopped and stared. If it wasn't for the fact that she'd disappoint Ryan, she'd have turned around and run all the way back to her car, probably never leaving her property again.

"Margaret, you're here!" Ryan called out. He jogged over to her, wearing a black baseball cap and a bright orange shirt. The sun was still out, the sky blue with thin clouds here and there. All in all, it was a pleasant evening.

She reached out and touched his arm. "Hey, yeah, wouldn't miss it. How does it feel to be fourteen? Oh, here. Before I forget, I got you something." She yanked out the wrapped knife and then cringed at the red bow she'd attached. How stupid was that for a boy?

To his credit, he didn't roll his eyes, but she could tell he wasn't impressed by the size of the frilly decoration.

"Open it," she said.

He started to pull the tape, but Joe shouted to him,

"Hey, Ryan, you know better. Put it with the other gifts until after."

"Sorry, Joe. That was my fault," Margaret stuttered, gazing awkwardly at the strangers and clasping her hands together for lack of anything better to do with them.

Ryan raced to a round plastic table outside the house, which had a few gifts stacked, and placed hers in the pile.

Joe nestled a beer between thumb and forefinger, took a swig, then waved at Margaret while he poked the guy barbequing beside him. The guy was tall, good looking, with broad shoulders, and he looked as good as Joe in a pair of blue jeans. He had short red hair, freckles and wore an Idaho Vandals t-shirt. Everyone there was in blue jeans, but then, in this part of the country, no one wore anything else. Good thing she had realized that before putting on something really stupid, like a skirt or, God forbid, a sundress.

This was the hardest thing she could remember ever having done—next to walking in and facing the hospital board to be fired, that is, which was one of her worst nightmares. It burned a hole in her stomach now as the memory of the experience flashed through her head. With her underarms damp, beads of sweat rolling down her back, she dug deep and took that next step, walking into this close group of people who didn't know her at all and made her feel about as welcome as a carpenter ant in a cedar house.

"Oh, Madeline, you made it?" It was Sara, who stepped out of Joe's small one-story house, which had blue shutters and a deck that wrapped around the front. She wore a dark pair of shorts, showing off slim, tanned legs, and a ruffled blue shirt. Her long blond hair was pinned up, with curls cascading down her back, and she looked to be in her early twenties.

Margaret cringed. Having someone forget your name was bad, but having it happen in front of a dozen strangers was worse. "Hi," she said.

The few lawn chairs on the grass were all taken by the women, clumped together in a circle, and all were staring at her. The men were standing, all with beers, and quick mental math let Margaret know she was the only single person here. Not good. No wonder the women stared. The men obviously knew better—more codes and rules she was sure to break. This was truly awful. Sara strode right to Joe, sliding her arm possessively up his. He leaned down and kissed her, and she linked their arms.

"Madeline, would you like a beer?" Sara asked. "Joe, aren't you going to introduce her to everyone?"

"Hi, Madeline," one of the women said. "My name's Nancy. I'm Vern's wife. He's that handsome guy barbequing with Joe." Nancy was sitting with the group of women. She wore a yellow shirt and had short, dark hair. She smiled brightly and waved.

"My name's Margaret," she said, and it came out sounding a little raspy. Nancy winced and pressed her hand to her chest, glancing sharply at Sara.

"I'm so sorry, Margaret. I heard you were working with Storm, doing all kinds of great things. That horse, I swear, was about to kill someone. Vern even said to Joe there was no hope for that horse. He told Joe to put him down before someone got hurt."

"There's always hope for a horse. Sometimes it's just about figuring out what went wrong, but it's always about people when it comes to horse problems. Horses are really just mirrors to a situation, and they react to you and what's going on in your life." Everyone stared at her, and the only thing she could hear was the sizzling of some meat on the barbeque. She could see Joe staring at her with a dark look she hadn't seen before, but it convinced her he definitely didn't want her there. Someone cleared their throat roughly. Maybe she should leave, she thought, as she realized what she'd said.

Ryan took that moment to jog back over. He was a welcome sight to Margaret, especially since he seemed happy. She turned to face him and touched his shoulder so she could give everyone her back. What could ever have possessed her to talk about the root of Storm's problems here, of all places? "You know, Ryan, I think I should go," she said, wincing when she saw his disappointment.

She wondered now, by Joe's reaction when she'd walked in, if maybe she hadn't been expected. Maybe Ryan hadn't told his dad she was coming? The way Joe treated her when they were alone was far different from the cold disinterest he showed now. She was glad she'd decided to pull on her jean jacket, because when she got nervous, she sweated worse than any man. Her underarms, her back, and, she was positive, her green shirt were wet in the most awkward of places.

"Listen, you have a great birthday," she continued. "I should really get back. I didn't do any work with Storm today." She saw his disappointment when his shoulders dipped and his excitement dimmed. "It'll be okay. You have friends here. You'll have fun tonight...."

Ryan glanced over her shoulder. Margaret could feel her back heating up and heard footsteps behind her. Her heart was pounding, and she swallowed the urge to bolt as her leg muscles tightened and she glanced to the line of trees at the edge of the driveway, which would hide her as she raced down the road to her parked car.

"Dad, Margaret said she's leaving," Ryan said. What made it worse, other than the few whispers, was that everyone appeared to be listening. She cringed inwardly, and she really wanted to crawl into a hole and die. Her face warmed. She knew she was blushing.

"Ryan, I just wanted to wish you a happy birthday and give you your present. Really, I should go...."

Joe came into her line of sight, Sara attached to his side as if they were glued together.

"Dad, tell her to stay, please," Ryan asked.

"Margaret, dinner's almost ready. Come on, stay. Ryan really wants you here," Joe said, but somehow it lacked any real conviction.

Sara pursed her lips, glanced up at Joe, and then patted his arm as she moved toward Margaret, sliding her hand around her elbow and linking their arms as if they were the best of friends, saying, "Yes, stay, please. Joe, get her a beer." Sara turned back to Margaret. "Look, there's so much food. Everyone brought something." Some of the women were now filling plates, and teens were crowding the food table filled with salads, buns, and beans.

A platter of hot dogs and burgers was set on the table by Vern as he shouted, "Burgers and dogs are ready! Everyone come and eat."

A plate was passed to Margaret, and everyone's attention was now on the food and, thankfully, not the fact that she was a social misfit. How did one go about learning the niceties of polite conversation? She'd have given anything for the sky to open up and grace her with something intelligent to say. But her tongue became thick and heavy and her mind went blank.

It was taking everything she had in her to fight the urge to drop her plate and run, which would ensure she'd never be able to show her face anywhere in this county again. It just wasn't an option, so she scooped up a few types of salads and dressed a burger, quelling the horrible shaking that had her nerves on edge.

Sara called to her and motioned her over. "Come and grab a seat!"

Margaret moved away from the table to find a spot to sit. She didn't like Sara, but she had to admit that she was the only one other than Ryan making any attempt with her at all.

"I don't want to take anyone's chair," Margaret said as she stared at several of the empty chairs the women had been sitting in.

Sara shook her head. "They're first come, first serve. Joe put them all out for everyone."

Margaret took the white plastic one beside Sara, and they were joined by the other women and a few husbands. Some of the men grabbed some lawn chairs from the back of a pickup and brought them over.

Nancy carried a plate of food and two open beers in her other hand. "Margaret, I don't think anyone has got you settled in with a beer yet."

Margaret realized she was probably supposed to have brought her own—and, from the spread, a side dish, too. "Oh, thank you. I didn't bring anything, and I don't really drink...."

"Oh, nonsense. This is a birthday party, and if there's one thing Joe's barbeques never have a shortage of, it's beer," Nancy added.

Margaret accepted the dark cold bottle of beer. "Thank you." She took a swallow of the bitter brew, thankful for the buzz it gave her, hoping it would at least boost her courage.

"Heard from Ryan that you've done some amazing things with Storm," Vern, Nancy's handsome redheaded husband, said. "There hasn't been anyone for a while around these parts who's worked with horses. Where did you learn to work with them, anyway?"

Margaret swallowed, because the way Vern watched her was familiar. "Grandpa always had horses," she said. "He was good with them, taught me a lot about how to listen to them, talk to them and be around them. Horses read every part of us and react to us. I've never had formal training, but Storm's done well. He's making progress. I'm building trust with him and hope to get him back to Ryan soon so he can start reconnecting. He needs to build trust with Storm and let go of his fear."

"Do you really think that's possible? I mean, I told Joe that horse has a mean look. I was here the last time he threw Ryan, and tried to stomp him."

Everyone was listening to Vern, even Joe, who lingered in the background and was watching Margaret with unwelcome hardness. Good grief, why had she ever agreed to come?

"I can only try. You know, when you step into that ring and there's something going on in your head, your horse is going to pick up on it and react to it," Margaret said before taking another swallow of beer. "You need to figure out who you are, and be comfortable in your own skin, before you get in that ring. With horses, you need to go slow and give them time. If they believe they're trapped, you need to first help them understand you're not confining them."

"Don't you mind living alone way out here?" Sara asked, daintily taking a bite of salad as if she hadn't heard a word Margaret had said. "I mean, what if something happened? Joe said you don't have a phone."

"No, I like it. I just haven't had a chance to hook up the phone, is all," she explained. *That asshole,* she thought. Why the hell was Joe telling Sara all about her business?

"Joe said you grew up and went to school here?" Sara said.

Margaret really didn't like the way this conversation

was going, because she thought Joe hadn't remembered her, or at least she hoped he hadn't. She didn't want to be remembered as the awkward misfit who had been teased mercilessly. "Yeah, I lived with my grandfather," she said.

"Oh, I knew I remembered you from school," one of the guys said. He had dark curly hair and a soft belly, and he was holding a burger, standing behind the overweight bleached blonde sitting across from her. "You were that tall girl. Remember, Joe? You called her Stretch. That was the first time we saw a girl we all had to crane our necks to look up to." The guy laughed, but Margaret wanted to cry inside. She'd hated that while growing up. The snickers, the laughter behind her back whenever she walked into a room or in class, all the ridiculous nicknames.

"Oh, please, Mike. You guys were all jealous, is all," Nancy barked at the round-faced man.

"Wow, I can't imagine," Sara said. "That must have been awful for you. I mean, for girls it's awkward enough, but Joe was telling me how you never fit in." She spoke softly and sounded genuinely caring.

Margaret could feel the hairs on the back of her neck doing their Spidey-sense warning thing. It was something she'd learned to pay attention to, and she would have given anything in that moment to crawl under her chair and hide. She couldn't shake the sense that things were about to get worse.

"Sara," Joe said, but she didn't look at him. She smiled at Margaret and then set her fork on her plate.

"Joe was just telling me about the time you turned up in class wearing a toque, and he yanked it off and your hair was bright orange, and your face went beet red. What was it you called her then, Joe, Carrot? Wasn't that what you told me?" Sara giggled as if it was the funniest thing.

Margaret cried inside and felt the ache in her jaw from

forcing a look on her face that said everything was fine. Yeah, she remembered trying to fit in, becoming a blonde, hoping that would be all it took for the guys to like her, maybe ask her out. She had failed miserably when the bleach turned her hair orange instead.

"Sara, that's enough," Joe barked, but Sara continued.

"Oh my, and then Joe said how everyone laughed at you, including the teacher, and every day you had to—"

"Sara," Joe interrupted, his tone filled with warning. Everyone was staring at Margaret, the men looking away awkwardly. Some blushed, another cleared his throat, and no one laughed now. It was one of those moments where she would have loved to be an ostrich and shove her head in a hole, but she couldn't. She sat frozen, her untouched dinner balanced on her lap.

"It was a home dye job that went bad," she said. "Thought I'd try blond. Didn't work, though, and my grandfather made me live with it. Going to school every day was my punishment until it grew out, all because I had used his peroxide without asking." She tipped back the last of the beer and stood up, staggering a bit. Her burger slid off the plate and landed on the ground, and she stared in horror. *Could it get any worse?* she wondered.

"Let me get that," Nancy said, grabbing the plate as Margaret bent over to get her burger.

"I'm sorry…" Margaret stuttered.

"Vern, get Margaret another burger. I'll give this to the dogs," Nancy said, tossing it in the grass.

"Thank you for inviting me, but I should go," Margaret began. She moved past everyone, Nancy beside her, and dumped the paper plate in the garbage by the table. Joe had pulled Sara away from the others, and he was holding her elbow. Whatever he was saying, she didn't seem happy, and he appeared even more unhappy.

"Margaret, stay," Nancy said. "Don't go. Don't mind Sara. I could never have believed how mean Joe was then, yanking off your hat.... That's horrible." Nancy stared at her with the first bit of remorse Margaret had seen from anyone here.

She winced and touched Nancy's hand. "No, I need to go. This is Ryan's party. Besides, I have work to do."

She hurried away before anyone could say something. Even though Nancy called after her, she kept going. As soon as she passed the line of trees on the driveway, hiding her from everyone, she started running. Letting all of her hurt drift away, she was relieved when she reached the end of the trail beside the mud bog, where her car was parked on the side of the road. She froze, slapping her hand to her side. Her keys were in the beige cloth purse she normally didn't carry, sitting under that plastic chair in Joe's front yard. She had two choices, suck it up and go back, in the biggest walk of shame she would ever experience, or walk the five miles home.

Margaret started walking.

Eight

J oe couldn't believe it. When he turned around, the damn woman had already taken off. Everyone was quiet, sitting with their mouths open, staring and shaking their heads.

Vern took a huge bite of his burger. "Spooks easily, doesn't she?" he mumbled.

Nancy smacked his arm and cast narrowed eyes at Sara and Joe. "She was embarrassed. For the life of me, I did some awful things growing up, but it's not right for an adult to embarrass someone like that. You're supposed to have some respect and understanding. You guys were awful to her in school," she said, crossing her arms and tossing the remains of Margaret's dinner into the garbage.

"Well, why's everyone looking at me? I thought what you told me was hilarious, Joe. Doesn't she have a sense of humor?" Sara said, as if she were the wounded party.

Joe couldn't believe the little chit. As he stared at her, he wondered what could have possessed her to blurt the story out in front of everyone. Maybe he shouldn't have shared with Sara the little he had known about Margaret in school, but he was ticked off at her and thought she needed to be knocked down a peg or two. Sara now had a look about her as if she was wondering why he was so mad. Well, hell, he was mad at himself for trusting her to be discreet. The only reason he had told her was that she made it too easy to share, but now he felt like crap, especially as he relived the wounded look in Margaret's eyes. No matter what he thought of her, he knew what Sara had said was cruel. He was just thankful he hadn't shared what Hazel had told him about Margaret being fired from her position as a prominent surgeon. No, there was something about it that would have made him embarrassed to mention it to anyone.

"Joe, is this her purse?" Nancy said, sliding back the plastic chair and holding up a beige cloth purse. Joe stared at the thing, because he didn't have a clue what she had brought. Nancy made a face. "You're such a guy. This is her purse, and you need to take it to her, or we could drop it off on our way home," she added, turning to her husband. "Someone should apologize to her."

Joe didn't know why, but he didn't like the idea of Nancy and Vern taking it back. After all, it was his place she'd run from and he felt responsible. He started shaking his head, and before he could stop himself, he said, "No, I'll take it."

"What?" Sara squeaked beside him. She flushed when he glanced at her, letting her know how annoyed he was. "Of course," she said then, touching his arm. "I'll come with you."

He wondered if his eyes bugged out of his head, as he heard someone chuckle behind him. "No. I'll run it over after we finish up here," he said.

Sara didn't say anything else, but she did slide her hand up his back and hook her arm in his. She leaned into him, all soft and curvy, and smiled.

Joe looked around at his friends and caught a glimpse of Ryan at the bottom of the steps, alone, watching the road where Margaret had gone. His son dumped his half-eaten plate on the table beside the gifts and went inside.

———

Margaret was just topping the hill, her driveway in view, when she heard a vehicle coming behind her. She glanced at the road and the narrow ditch, turning to see who was coming, and froze as a sudden jolt tore through her. It was Joe and his damn truck, dust flying. He had obviously spotted her, as he slowed and then pulled off to the side. He jumped out, the engine still running, and Margaret stood and watched as he came around the front of the truck. He stared down at her with a look that was irritated, dark, and filled with something else that had her quelling the panic that was starting to choke off her next breath.

He set his hand on his hip and then shook his head. "You plan on walking all the way home? I suppose your car keys are in that purse you left behind before you ran out."

Margaret swallowed and glanced up at the truck, letting out a sigh of relief when she realized no one was with him, namely the blonde who had just ground her into the dirt. She opened her mouth to speak, but not a sound came out.

"Get in," he said, setting his hand out toward her as if she'd spook and bolt the other way. He gestured toward the passenger door and moved her with his large body as if she was being herded. He pulled open her door and all but tossed her in, slamming the door shut and walking around.

Margaret touched her cloth purse in the middle of the seat and set her hand on the door when he jumped in. His sharp gaze didn't miss a thing, as he raised his eyebrows and said, "You planning on running again?"

She dropped her hand into her lap and had just reached for the seatbelt when Joe spun the truck around, going the other direction.

"Joe, look…" she started, but she stopped when he gave her a sharp glance.

"Look, I'm sorry about what Sara said," he began. "That wasn't okay, but I can't believe you ran like that and left your car parked on the side of the road to walk. Why wouldn't you come back for your keys?"

"I was embarrassed, okay? I shouldn't have come to Ryan's party. I realized I probably wasn't expected. He didn't tell you he had invited me, did he?" she said, watching the way he ran his hand over his chin, obviously trying to hide his discomfort.

He kicked up the gas and didn't answer. Margaret looked away. Why would he have told Sara about her nightmarish teenage years? She'd hated every minute of growing up as a gangly misfit whose only joy was coming home and talking to her horse. Snow, a gelding, was a palomino cross who had died before she left for medical school. She squeezed her eyes shut at the ache that came from nowhere and sucker punched her. Snow's death was a loss she had never gotten over.

She heard Joe clear his throat. "I heard that something happened in Seattle and you lost your job," he said before clearing his throat again.

Margaret realized then that the horror and embarrassment that had been flung in her face by Joe's girlfriend had nothing on this. How the hell had he found out, anyway? She hadn't told anyone, slinking back here to hide. She felt the tingle of a heated blush flood her cheeks, and when she glanced in horror at Joe, he must have seen how freaked out she was. He reached across the seat and touched her arm.

"Hey, I'm sorry. It's not the end of the world."

She couldn't believe he'd said that. "Not the end of the world, are you kidding? I screwed up. Tell that to a little boy and his family. Who told you, anyway?"

She shut her eyes. It had to have been Hazel. Stan and Hazel, friends of her grandfather, had been like surrogate parents for her while she was growing up. The day she'd come back to Post Falls, she had promised herself she would never tell anyone, but Hazel and Stan had arrived with a casserole, a pound cake and questions aplenty. Hazel had started asking when Margaret had to be back at the hospital, and she just wouldn't let it drop, though she could obviously read Margaret's body language and see how upset she was. Well, it had come pouring out. She'd never been good at hiding anything.

Her face was burning as she stared out of the passenger window, praying Joe would drive faster so she could jump out of the truck, climb into her car and drive away. Instead, he pulled to the side and stopped.

"Hey, what are you doing?" she said, almost jumping as she slid around in her seat to face Joe. He shoved the gearshift into park.

"Look, Hazel didn't mean anything by it. I think she was worried, is all. I can only imagine how you're feeling. Did you do it intentionally?"

She couldn't believe he would ask something like that.

"Oh my God, of course not! What would ever make you think something like that?" She knew she must sound exasperated, but she couldn't understand how he could say something so awful, so cruel, so… She stopped when she saw a familiar twinkle in his eyes. "You're a jerk."

"Maybe, but I'm glad to hear you understand it wasn't intentional. I may not know much about being a doctor or, pardon, a fancy surgeon, but I'm pretty sure you're human just like the rest of us. You make mistakes, too." He was watching her with far too much concern, a familiarity they didn't share, or so she needed to tell herself. She rubbed her arms.

"Tell that to the little boy who'll be stuck in a nightmare for the rest of his life, unable to recognize anyone. His parents suddenly have a stranger for a son. No, I deserve what happened. If I could trade places with him…" She shook her head, feeling a familiar overwhelming numbness. That place she'd gone too often, when the pain and guilt of what she'd done became too much. "Could you drive me to my car, please? I'd like to go home," she said. She couldn't look at him but could feel the heat from his gaze, and she shut her eyes, keeping her gaze averted, praying he wouldn't say another word. Finally, he started the truck, shoved it into gear, and started driving.

He pulled in front of her car and had barely stopped when she jumped out and froze, realizing she had left her purse again. This time, when she turned to reach for it, he leaned across and handed it to her. She didn't miss the softness—or was it understanding?—in his expression.

"Don't be kind to me," she said, shutting the door before he could say another word. She hurried to her car just as a truck pulled out of Joe's, honking its horn, someone yelling out at her as she slid into her car and shut the door. She didn't think as she started the engine, glanced to the side and pulled out in front of the green truck without a wave or a honk or anything, but her eyes did lock on to Joe's as he watched her drive away.

Margaret was still in bed, listening to the birds chirping. Storm and Angel were neighing softly in answer. She'd tossed and turned most of the night, sleeping in fits, waking almost every hour, and now her head felt like a lead weight from the lack of sleep.

Her eyes felt thick and heavy from the tears she'd shed all night as she relived the horror of the botched surgery on that little boy. It had been a nick, a fraction off, just barely, but she knew she'd screwed up as soon as she made the cut. She'd gone through the procedure again and again, over and over, at least a hundred times in her head, reliving the nightmare, trying as she might to figure out why her overconfidence had made her screw up so badly. She'd outlined the surgery, all the steps. She'd had it down, or she should have, anyway. She rubbed her face with her hand as she wondered where that eight-year-old boy was now. Was he in rehab or at home? She thought of the struggles his parents were now having.

She heard the deep purr of a truck, Joe's truck, and she instantly jolted and leaped from bed, wearing only a thin nightshirt that barely covered her thighs. She listened to the door slam, footsteps in the dirt, and frantically searched for a shirt, pants, anything to pull on. She grabbed the jeans she had tossed in a heap on the floor and stepped into them just as she heard footsteps on her porch and a knock at her door.

"Margaret, it's Joe," he yelled out.

She grabbed a sweater tossed over the foot of her bed and shrugged it on, hurrying barefoot to the front door, catching a glimpse of bed hair in the mirror and smudges from the previous night's makeup under her eyes.

He pounded on the door again. "Open the door, Margaret, or I'm coming in."

She heard the locked doorknob jangle and watched in horror as the door shook. He really was trying to come in. She pulled her sweater closed over her breasts and pulled open the door, peeking out at Joe with the door in front of her as a shield. Dammit, the man looked good in a tan barn coat, ratty cowboy hat, and dark whiskers as if he hadn't bothered to shave that morning.

He took in her attire, and Margaret couldn't help the wave of self-consciousness that passed through her. She ran her hand over her tangled hair, and her sweater gaped, her bare feet feeling the chill. She grabbed the edges of her sweater, feeling her face warm.

Joe set his hand on her door, and her gaze went to it. "Just in case you try to slam the door in my face," he said.

"I'm sorry. I was still in bed. I didn't sleep well last night," she said. She could smell his scent, and it was so warm and enticing that it rattled her nerves.

"Got any coffee?" he asked.

"I haven't made any yet." She gestured behind her, and Joe took a step inside, crowding her and forcing her back. He took in the empty living room.

"Why don't you get dressed, and I'll put some coffee on, if you don't mind me rummaging through your kitchen?" he said.

She realized he wasn't really asking her. In fact, he stepped inside and shut the door as she stepped back again.

"Joe, I'm…" she started. She didn't know why he was here, and she was still embarrassed—hell, not embarrassed, mortified—from the previous night and how she had behaved.

"The coffee's where?" he asked, walking into the small walkthrough kitchen. She cringed because she had next to nothing for food and a sink full of dirty dishes that had piled up over the past two days. When it came to housework, she would rather shovel out a barn than set foot in a kitchen.

She heard him stop and then turn, raising his eyebrow as he looked at the mess. She shrugged. "Sorry, it's kind of a disaster."

He didn't seem to dwell on it, chuckling and shaking his head. "You're kind of an enigma. I somehow pictured your place neat and tidy, with frilly decorations and useless knickknacks," he said. He yanked open a cupboard and then another before taking the red coffee can out. He pulled out the used coffee filter and opened the cupboard under her sink. "You got a garbage?"

Margaret stepped closer and pointed. "That pail under there. Just dump it in. I haven't picked up any garbage bags, either," she said. She took another step as she watched him dump some water in her coffee pot, measure out some grounds, and flick it on. "You really see me as the kind of person with frilly knickknacks and…?" She stopped talking as she took in the sparseness of the place as if seeing it for the first time.

"What happened to all the furniture?" Joe asked.

"It had to go, broken-down crap. It kind of spooked me a bit, too. Granddad was found dead in his favorite chair, so that had to go, and it was just stuff, anyway. It doesn't mean much to me." She stepped closer again as she watched him frown. "I don't like frilly things, Joe, and I don't have much use for fancy trinkets. The best gift I ever got was a box set with a cordless drill, a jigsaw and a chop saw. I was fifteen, and that was my Christmas present. Granddad didn't waste time buying me girly stuff. I remember I made cut-outs of horses and helped Granddad build that potting shed out back. It was the best Christmas ever."

His face softened as he listened to her.

Margaret shrugged as she remembered how well her grandfather had known her. She loved to work with her hands, building, cutting, and maybe that was why he hadn't been surprised when she told him she wanted to be a surgeon.

"I didn't know that about you," Joe said. She shrugged, running her fingers through her tangled hair, and the coffeemaker beeped. Joe turned to the pot. "You got some mugs, anything clean?" he asked in a teasing way that did, in fact, lighten the mood.

"I sure hope so," she said. She didn't know for sure, and she looked at the pile of dishes as Joe opened cupboard doors and then held up a chipped blue mug and a larger brown one. "Sorry about this mess. I'm not much good at housework," she said, accepting the mug of coffee after Joe poured her the larger cup. She took a sip and was grateful, as she breathed in the strong aroma, that it helped to clear the cobwebs in her head. She wondered if he thought she needed more caffeine.

"Any milk?" he asked, and she started to gesture to the fridge before wincing.

"Probably not," she said. He dropped his hand just as it touched the fridge door. "Are you okay without it?" she asked as he picked up the chipped mug and took a sip.

"Yeah, I'll be fine." He paused. "You have a great smile."

She realized he had lightened the mood and made her feel a little better, but she didn't have a clue how to take a compliment, so she gestured to her cup. "Good coffee, thank you. Can't remember the last time someone made me a cup in my own kitchen."

"So, about last night," he said. "I know you were pretty upset about me knowing you were fired. You've got to shake it off, Margaret, and forgive yourself. We all make mistakes. God knows I've made my share."

She firmed her lips and said, "I think there might be a difference between me costing a boy his future and, I don't know, you making fun of someone."

He bristled at her response, and she couldn't help but notice the twitch in his cheek and the way a white line formed on his lips from holding them tight. "Would you please get the stick out of your ass?" he snapped.

"What?" she sputtered.

"Don't go taking that the wrong way, as well. Yes, what you did is pretty shitty, but I'm sure you've beaten yourself up far more than those docs or corporate yahoos who fired your ass ever could." He took another step closer to Margaret as she watched him over the rim of her cup. "You said you wanted to trade places with that kid. Well, I've been exactly where you are."

She frowned at that and wondered what he meant. She gestured and started to ask when he blurted out, "My wife."

She lowered her cup, because one thing she did know was that Joe's wife had died, and she could see the shadow of pain, something she was all too familiar with, flicker in his expression.

"I'm sorry, Joe. Sometimes I say things I shouldn't, especially with you."

Well, that had his attention. He nodded.

"What happened to your wife?"

He didn't say anything for the longest time.

"You know, you don't have to tell me. It's none of my business...."

"It was my fault." He cut her off, and from the way he said it, she could hear how he felt responsible.

She wanted to reach out and touch his arm, to tell him it would be okay, that it wasn't his fault, but she said none of it because she didn't know what had happened. She just held the hot mug as he glanced at the floor, obviously trying to gather his courage to say something.

"Evie, she'd been having some women's problems, cramping, and she ignored it. Actually, she didn't make a big deal about it because I'd been laid off from the mill. We had no insurance, so going to the doctor...we had no money." He let out a mournful sigh. "You've probably heard that a thousand times."

She just watched him, because she knew where this was going. He was right. She'd gotten mad—no, furious—at the many patients who ignored their symptoms for something treatable until it was too late, and it always came down to money, insurance, HMOs.

"It was two years before she started losing weight. I thought at first that she was trying to, and then one day she doubled over in pain. I rushed her into the emergency room. They did some tests, and then a specialist came in and said it was cancer, late-stage cervical cancer that had spread to her lungs, her stomach, her liver…"

Margaret shut her eyes, because that was a death sentence. "How long?"

He must have known what she was asking, as he said, "She died two weeks later." He dumped out the rest of his coffee and set it on the counter. "I'm pretty sure you don't hold the corner on the pity party. Evie didn't go to the doctor because she didn't want to add to my worries. Docs cost a lot, and we were struggling, but I would have sold my soul to the devil to pay. I've relived what that doctor said over and over millions of times in my head. If she'd seen a doctor, had an annual checkup, a pap smear, they'd have caught it sooner, and it would have been treatable, a different outcome. She'd still be here, and I'd still have my wife."

"Joe, you didn't know," Margaret said.

"Well, that's the thing. Deep down, I knew something was wrong, but she made it easier by telling me not to worry, that everything would be fine. I took the coward's way out." He stepped closer to her. "Give yourself a break. At least you tried," he said. He touched her arm and then stepped around her to the door, opening it. "Do you want me to feed your horses? It looks like Storm is about to wear a hole in the dirt where he's pacing."

She watched him. He was such an enigma, and she was seeing a side of him she hadn't known existed. He'd exposed a dark part of himself to help her feel better, and she could see how he was struggling with a pain he doubted could ever go away.

"Joe, thank you," she said.

He didn't turn to face her but inclined his head as he stepped out of the house. She didn't miss the hardness in his jaw and the way he was struggling to hold himself together, and, for the first time, she felt something deep and close. It was as if he'd cut through her tough outer shell, cracking open her heart and touching her. Warmth flooded her in a rush as she watched him step out of the house and take care of her horses. There was something simple about it, and she couldn't shake the deep longing she felt, wondering what it would be like to be cared for by him. She realized how badly she yearned for that very thing.

J oe spent his day putting out one fire after the other. First, the well pump broke, so there was no water to the house. After spending all day fixing it, he had no time to mill wood, and he needed to finish the order for a new contractor who was building a mile up the road. He was just wiping his hands and turning on the power to the working pump when Ryan came walking up the road with this backpack looped over his shoulder. "Hey, Ryan. How was school today?" Joe asked.

"Good," Ryan said, shrugging his shoulders. It was the same response he gave every day.

"Any homework?" Joe asked, knowing exactly what was coming.

"No."

He watched Ryan saunter to the house. "So if I call your teacher, she'll tell me the same thing?"

Ryan stopped and seemed to hesitate before looking up at Joe. The way his eyes searched out the dead air, he was either trying to come up with a story or thinking of what really had gone down that day. The teacher usually described Ryan's work with two words: "incomplete" and "sloppy."

"Of course she will," Ryan said with a frown. "Can I go see Margaret and Storm?"

Joe shook his head, wanting to take his son by the shoulders and give him a good shake. The fact was that Ryan hated school. He was a smart kid, but sitting at a desk, being made to listen for hours on end, did little to inspire him. Joe had hated that about school, as well. Maybe that was why he'd cut Ryan some slack, but now he thought maybe all his son needed was some female influence. He'd wondered a lot lately about Evie. If she were still alive, what kind of guidance would she have given his son? Joe was sure Ryan would be a lot more focused in school.

"You know, Ryan, you're growing up, and slacking off isn't going to get you anywhere in life. You need an education, and I can't be hounding you every day about whether you did your homework or took an interest in school. You need to take initiative. You're not two years old. I can't make you do it," he said. He was irritated about a whole lot of things, and now Ryan was shuffling from foot to foot.

"Can I go see Storm?" he asked again.

Joe let out a sigh. Ever since he'd gone to see Margaret that morning, intent on somehow making her feel better, he had felt miserable, as if he'd traded places with her. He couldn't help resenting Margaret, as she was responsible for his mood, even though he knew it wasn't logical. "Fine, go," he said, "but be back for dinner."

Ryan hesitated and then got a hopeful look on his face. "Do you want to come with me? I'm sure Margaret would be happy to see you."

Joe saw something in his son's eyes that he didn't like. Ryan would have been a fool not to pick up on the interest

Joe had for Margaret, and, in a way, Joe wondered if his son was looking at her as a replacement for Evie.

"You're not trying to matchmake, there, are you, son? I hope not, because you'll be really disappointed. I have a girlfriend, Sara. I like her, and she likes you."

Ryan made a face. "She does not," he said. He walked away and dumped his backpack in the house before racing to his bike.

"Ryan, helmet!" Joe yelled out as Ryan started down the driveway. He turned back and grabbed his yellow helmet from a hook in the shed before jumping on his bike again. "Don't be late," Joe called out just as Ryan disappeared behind the line of trees down the driveway.

―――――

Margaret hadn't missed the differences between Angel and Storm. Storm didn't like treats and was standoffish, letting her know he expected to be left alone. Angel was a different story. She raced across the paddock or corral to Margaret every time she stepped in. Margaret only had to call to Angel for the horse to give her all her attention. She loved treats and would eat out of Margaret's hand, whereas with Storm, Margaret had to be careful not to get bitten. Where Angel was calm and had an energy that matched Margaret's, Storm was definitely the polar opposite. He had an energy and personality that she could see wasn't suited for Ryan.

Margaret had seen the boy's fear of Storm, and the horse was now feeding off it, or so she suspected. She had to become strong around Storm to get a response from him and get him to think, to work. Today, she'd worked his hind quarters like a clock. Angel was spatially aware, so Margaret was never worried about getting kicked. With

Storm, though, she was ever mindful of her location behind him.

She tossed a flake of hay into the feeder for both horses and then turned as she heard Ryan pulling up on his bike. She realized she needed to speak with Joe about the horse.

"How's Storm today?" he asked, sounding hopeful as he dropped his bike in the middle of the driveway and joined her at the corral.

She touched his arm and watched as he gazed at his horse with something hopeful and hesitant in his eyes. "You love Storm, don't you?" she asked, mainly to see his reaction.

"Of course! He's my horse. I just want to feel comfortable with him. Did you work out whatever his problem is?"

She studied Ryan and wondered how to address the real issue. Storm really needed someone with a skill level to match his own energy, and she doubted Ryan would ever be the right fit. She could be wrong. Maybe it was just a matter of working with Ryan and helping him gain skill and confidence. That could work, or it could get him killed.

"Ryan, with horses, no two are the same, just like with people. There are mismatched personalities, energy levels. You can't change who a horse is. A horse that's forward and excitable isn't going to be good for someone who wants a slow, easy ride. You'll be fighting with the horse the entire way. It's the same with someone who wants excitement and drive. They'd get pretty frustrated with an easygoing horse who would rather pick its way at a nice, calm pace. These kinds of differences frustrate the horse and the rider."

"But you had me and Storm working together," Ryan added, frowning.

"And I can keep working with you and Storm. I just

need to make sure your personalities are matched. Just like with people, some are born to go fast and thrive on challenges, taking risks, while some can't handle that and need to play it safe. Storm has a strong personality, and when you're with him, you need to make yourself bigger, stronger. Your energy has to come from here." She patted her stomach. "You need to be really clear with Storm, when you enter that arena, about exactly what your expectation is. All the emotion, the worry and the problems you have in here," she tapped her forehead, "need to be hidden away somewhere else. We're emotional beings. Horses aren't, but they will react to our emotions."

She watched Ryan. He seemed to hesitate and think.

"I'm not ready to give up on Storm," he said.

"Okay then. Let's get you in the round pen with him——" She stopped when she heard a familiar engine from her driveway. Joe's truck appeared, and she felt her heart leap until she spotted the blonde who, just last night, had humiliated her in front of a bunch of people she barely knew.

Joe stopped in front of the bike Ryan had dumped in the middle of the road. He shut off the engine and climbed out, holding a hand out to Sara and helping her down. She had cascading curls and wore dark blue jeans with a deep green shirt. Her belt buckle flashed with something sparkly. The woman was holding Joe's hand, beaming with the brightest smile.

Joe, though, stopped at the bike and picked it up. "Ryan, how many times have I told you not to leave your bike lying around?" He hefted the bike into the back of the truck.

"Dad, I was just going to do some work in the round pen with Storm," Ryan said with a whine in his voice, one she heard only when his dad was around and he was on the defensive.

"Not tonight," Joe said. "Sara's making us dinner, and we have some news we want to share."

Margaret gripped the wood rail of the corral when she saw the way Sara sucked in her lower lip and fluttered her lashes up at Joe. She walked toward him as he held his hand out to her, and she pressed every part of herself up against him. Joe set a kiss to her forehead. If there had ever been any doubt about how intimate and close the two were, there was no doubt now, not in Margaret's mind. Whatever had happened this morning between them… well, she felt like an ass. How could she misread things so badly, and why did he have to be kind to her?

The happy couple was watching both Ryan and Margaret, and Ryan didn't seem interested in having any part of their happy news. In fact, he refused to ask. Margaret was with Ryan one hundred and fifty percent. She wasn't interested in learning one iota of what they thought was happy, because right now, her stomach was doing that Spidey-sense thing that made her want to run as far and fast as she could before Joe said one more word.

"We're getting married," he said before kissing Sara.

Margaret's ears were ringing, and Ryan made a sound as if he'd been sucker punched. She didn't know what to do. Could she manage to congratulate them? Being happy for them definitely wasn't a possibility. What she did do was set her hand on Ryan's shoulder and say, "You'd best go on home with your dad."

The look Ryan gave her then, his eyes glistening with tears, nearly broke her heart.

argaret had never been so inspired to scrub her house from one end to the other. It wasn't the fact that she wanted it to look nice so much that she felt nothing at all. She was hurt and feeling as if she was worthless, and she had to do something to keep from going out of her mind. She kept replaying Joe's visit. Why had he told her about his wife? He had seemed so concerned about how she was feeling, about how she had messed up the surgery for Charlie, that little boy, whose future was now uncertain. Was Joe concerned that she was blaming herself? Instead of feeling better, which Joe had been solely responsible for, she now felt unlovable. She didn't know which feeling was worse, her overwhelming guilt or this. She dropped the sponge in the now spotless sink when a knock on her door had her glancing at the clock. It was after midnight.

She started to worry instantly. She didn't have a phone, and who would be out here, in the middle of nowhere, this late at night? She wondered why she hadn't heard anything outside. Storm, at least, would have startled at an intruder.

Margaret stepped closer to the door, her heart hammering as she stared at the unlocked deadbolt. The pounding rattled the door frame as if someone was using his fist on the door.

"Margaret!"

It was Joe, and she instantly felt relief—and fury. Why was he bothering her now?

She yanked open the door and stared into darkness before flicking on the outside light, but nothing happened. The damn bulb was dead, and she had never noticed because she never had much need to run out in the middle of the night. "Joe, you scared the life out of me," she said.

He stepped around her inside the house, water dripping from his slicker and the brim of his hat. She realized that was why she hadn't heard anything. It was pouring rain, and she saw the headlights from Joe's truck, still running.

"Is Ryan here?" he asked, his tone holding nothing friendly.

"No. He left with you and…" she started to say "Sara," but the woman's name left a bitterness on her tongue, and she couldn't get it past her lips. Joe shook his head as he took off his hat. He wore a look that was starting to spark fear in her. "Joe, what happened?" she said.

Joe shook his head. "I don't know. Ryan took off."

"When?" she asked. She knew how upset Ryan had been when his dad shared the news about him and Sara. She had understood the look he wore: dark, desperate and so alone.

"Sometime after nine," Joe said. "We had gone to bed, and I got up about an hour ago to check on him, but I found two pillows stuffed under his quilt. I looked everywhere for him. He's gone. His bike is nowhere to be found, and I thought maybe he came here." He was dripping on the rough hardwood floor, and Margaret shut the door. "Look, I'm sorry to bother you," he said, starting toward the door.

She wanted to kick him, because he was putting distance between them and making her feel as if Ryan wasn't her concern. She sighed and reached for her slicker, shrugging it on.

"What are you doing?" he asked as she shoved her feet into her gumboots and set the ratty hat she always wore on her head.

"Coming to help you find Ryan," she replied. "Any idea where he'd go?" She didn't ask why he had left, because she had a pretty good idea why. She wondered whether Joe had a clue how his son really felt about Sara. She pulled open the door and stepped out, Joe right behind her. "Joe, there's a flashlight in the closet there. Can you grab it?"

He stepped back in and opened the small coat closet, lifting the large flashlight from the shelf. He flicked it on but didn't hand it to Margaret when she reached for it, instead shining it toward his truck and pulling the door closed behind them. He jumped off the steps, starting toward his truck, and Margaret hurried after him. He wasn't about to wait for anyone.

She jumped into the passenger side, and he set her flashlight between them and backed up. They were turning to leave when the headlights flashed on Ryan's bike, leaning against the barn.

"Joe!" Margaret said, pointing just as he stomped on the brakes.

He was out the driver's door, yelling, "Ryan!" He cupped his hands around his mouth and shouted again. "Ryan, answer me now!"

Oh, he was mad and worried, and he would probably

kick Ryan's butt from one side of this county to the next when he found him—or maybe that was just what Margaret's grandfather would have done to her.

Margaret grabbed the flashlight and jumped out of the truck, starting toward the bike. Angel was under the overhang, doing her best to keep dry, and Margaret saw the open gate. She flashed the light on it and then into the corral. "Joe!" she called out as she walked toward the gate, which was now swinging back and forth in the wind. "Storm's gone," she said. She could hear the panic in her voice. "What the hell did Ryan do?"

She quickly shut the gate and latched the chain, not that Angel would go anywhere, but Storm…

Joe jogged over. "What?" He sounded so annoyed. "I don't care about that horse. I care about my son."

She ground her teeth and fought the urge to shove his arm, to yell at him and give him the dressing-down he so deserved. She glared at him as she stepped around him to the barn, where Ryan's bike was, and then inside. Storm's halter was gone, and so were the saddle and blanket she had for Angel. Her grandfather's old, heavy saddle was there, though. She let out a breath. "Oh my God, Ryan, what did you do?"

Joe was beside her. "What is it?" he asked.

Margaret shut her eyes, trying to figure out what to say, before she glanced at Joe. "My saddle is gone. So's the halter for Storm." She shone the light at another empty peg. "The bridle I used to use for Angel is gone, too."

Joe stepped in front of her, looking at her with something resembling blame. "Are you telling me my kid showed up here and saddled Storm, and you didn't hear anything?"

"You're not putting this on me," she snapped. "If you haven't noticed, it's raining. I didn't even hear you pull in. I was kind of busy inside." She stopped just short of telling him she'd been sulking, scrubbing down one end of the house to the other. He didn't need to know any of that. "If I recall, Ryan was none too thrilled by your news, so if you want to cast blame on someone, shine it right on yourself. You wanting to marry Sara is your business, but in case you didn't notice, Ryan doesn't like her, and he believes the feeling is mutual."

Joe ground his jaw and let out a low, gruff laugh that was anything but happy. "You're unbelievable. You're just jealous, and who I marry is none of your damn business," he snapped.

Margaret felt her jaw slacken, and she fisted her hand around the flashlight, wondering for a second what it would feel like to bash Joe over the head. Out of nowhere, she felt tears burning behind her eyes at his cruel words. "You can be a real prick sometimes, Joe. I care about Ryan very much."

Joe looked away and then said, "I'm sorry. I'm just worried about my kid. It's one of the reasons I asked Sara to marry me. He needs a mother."

She shone her light into his face, and he blinked, holding his palm up to shield his eyes.

"What the hell is the matter with you, woman?"

"You're an idiot," she said. "You don't marry someone to give your son a mother. In case you hadn't noticed, Sara is about as interested in being a mother to Ryan as a snake is to a mouse."

He didn't say a word as Margaret walked away, shining the light on the ground, searching for tracks or anything that would give her a clue as to where Ryan had gone. Joe reached for her flashlight and tried to grab it from her hand. "Hey, stop it, Joe!"

"What are you doing?" he snapped.

Maybe she should have worried she'd gone too far with what she'd said, but she didn't care, not right now. In fact, she felt a bit of fire that made her glad she'd been so sharp. Maybe he needed to hear it. After all, she wondered what part of his anatomy he'd been thinking with when he proposed marriage to Sara.

He reached again for her flashlight, this time snagging it in his hand and pulling her back to him.

"Joe, I'm trying to see the tracks!" she shouted at him.

He stepped around her, shining the light on the muddy ground. The rain puddled around the tracks, and she could feel a chill in the damp night air as she shivered.

"This way. Shine the light over here," she said, pointing to the path that led around the corral. She kept up with Joe as he started following the tracks to the edge of the forest. It was a trail that had been used by her grandfather to lead the cattle to the grassy knolls where they free ranged. The trails went back into hundreds of miles of wilderness. Joe stopped just at the edge of the path and shouted, "Ryan!"

There was nothing but the sound of the wind and the rain pounding the ground.

Twelve

Joe left Margaret standing at the edge of the clearing with the flashlight as he walked away. He was still reeling from what she had said to him about Sara. He thought she was a spiteful, jealous bitch, but he was embarrassed to admit she had nailed part of her analogy right on the head. That pissed him off more than anything, as he didn't want to admit that she could be right.

"Joe, where are you going?" she called out. He could hear her rubber boots slapping in the mud as she ran up behind him, but he didn't look back. He couldn't look at her, because she was making him think this was all his fault. He shoved her passenger door closed and strode around the front of his running truck.

"Joe, stop!" she shouted again, this time grabbing his arm and not letting go.

He glared at her, and she seemed to stand taller as she stood up to him. He knew his look should have had her taking a step back, putting as much distance between them as she could, but she was no pushover. She was about as different from Sara and Evie as any woman could get.

"Look, unless you're going to let me take your horse and go after my son, I need to hurry home and get mine. I'll be back, and then I'm going after my kid," he said.

This time, she let go of his arm and stepped back. "Fine, go," she said as she stepped away again.

Joe didn't wait. He slid behind the wheel and spun the tires, swinging the truck around and skidding in the mud as he raced back down the driveway, cursing the entire way and wondering what foolish notion could have gone through his son's head to make him believe this was a good idea.

When he pulled back in, the front door opened and Sara raced out with her jacket over her head. "Did you find him?" she called.

He slammed his door and leaped up the front steps into the house.

"Joe, you're tracking mud on the floor!" she said as he hurried into his bedroom and took in the queen-size bed, the olive-green sheets left in a rumpled disarray where he'd spent a couple of hours easing his need in the most sexy, responsive woman he'd ever had the good fortune to bed. What had his son done while he'd been in here, rutting like an animal? He'd stolen away into the night.

"I don't give a crap about the floor," Joe snapped. "I only care about my son." He pulled a wool sweater from his closet, dumped his slicker and hat on the bed, and pulled it on over his shirt. His jeans were damp from the rain, but he wasn't wasting any more time changing.

Sara snatched the wet garments off the bed and made a face. He took the slicker from her and wondered if she was more concerned about the mud and dirt than his son. With that thought came the memory of Margaret's cruel dressing-down, when she had all but insinuated that he was thinking with his dick instead of considering what was best for his son.

He set the damp hat on his head, and Sara sucked out her bottom lip. Every time she did that, it weakened his knees, and when she reached up on her tiptoes to kiss him, he gave her a light peck and then stepped around her.

"Joe, where are you going?" she said. She was on his heels, dogging him.

"To find my son. He took the horse from Margaret's and headed out onto one of the trails in the dark. Fool kid! I'm going after him."

"Joe, it's too dark out. Wait until morning, until it's light," she said.

"No," he snapped, and he gave her only a passing glance as he shook his head, pulling open the hall closet, where he kept his backpack and some gear for when he went into the bush. He froze and took in the neat and tidy shelves. The towels, sheets, and blankets that had been shoved in there were now folded neatly and sorted in an orderly fashion. He started rummaging. "Where's my backpack? I had a tarp folded in here, too, and my pocket saw…"

"Joe, stop. I just organized and moved all that junk out. I put it in a box in your garage. I can't believe you would have stuff like that inside," she said.

Right now, Joe wanted to wrap his hands around her neck and give her a shake. "I don't have time for this!" he snapped, striding to the attached garage, which was filled with junk and an old 75 Chevelle he planned to restore one day. "Bag up some food for me," he told her. "I don't know how long it will take me to find Ryan."

As he strode to the garage, he didn't miss the hiss of something, whether it was irritation or annoyance, from

Sara as she stomped into the kitchen, hopefully to do what he'd asked.

It took Joe twenty minutes to grab his backpack, tarp, flashlight, pocket knife, and some rope. He tossed every-thing, including some blankets, into the horse trailer, loading his palomino, Mercedes, in. Sara came out as he closed up the gate and handed him a bag.

"There's a couple sandwiches, a bottle of water, and some snacks," she said. She touched his arm. "Joe, I hope you find Ryan. Hurry home."

"Thank you," he muttered. He set the bag on the front seat and climbed in, driving away without another word.

It was pitch black when he drove back down Margaret's driveway over the ruts, hauling the trailer in, and his headlights flashed on her horse, saddled with what looked like gear or a tarp tied behind it. There was a light on outside the barn.

He shoved the truck in park and went around to open the trailer, leading out Mercedes and tying him to the post close to Margaret's horse.

"What are you doing?" he said as Margaret went around her horse, tightening the cinch.

"I'm going with you," she said.

"Woman, I don't have time to be babysitting you out there. I'm going to be moving fast," he snapped as he stomped away, opening the side trailer door, carting out the blanket and saddle for his horse. He just about stepped on Margaret when he turned around.

"I'm still going with you. For one, I'm the last person you'd have to babysit. Neither you or Ryan should be around Storm. I still can't believe Ryan took him and saddled him all by himself. He must have been desperate as all hell, Joe, to stoop to that. He's still terrified of that horse, and that tells me a lot about his state of mind. No, Joe, I know these backwoods very well." She reached inside the trailer and snatched the bridle for the palomino. Neither said a word as they saddled his horse.

When he climbed into the saddle, his backpack on his back and his gear wrapped in a tarp tied behind him, he faced Margaret in the dark as she walked her horse forward. "You want to take the lead? It's pretty dark still," he said.

She extended the large beam flashlight, and he took it.

"Stay close," he said. Then he turned his horse and guided it to the trail, the light bouncing on the ground as he looked for any sign of tracks. The pouring rain was quickly washing away any traces of where his son had gone.

———

Margaret followed Joe for what felt like hours. She could sense his frustration, his worry, and could hear the hoarseness in his voice as he called out to Ryan hundreds of times.

His horse slipped in the mud a couple times when they went up the slope of one of the trails that headed higher into the hills. Light had just begun to tip over the horizon, and shades of red cut through the clouds as the rain started to taper off. Margaret could feel the mist from all the wet, and she listened to the early morning sounds of life in the forest.

"Joe, there's a stream up ahead. We need to give the horses some water and a break."

"No, we need to keep moving," he snapped. She could

see that he'd easily run that horse into the ground unless someone reasoned with him.

"Joe, that horse is going to drop unless you give him a break, and then where will you be? Let them graze for a bit, and we can figure out where to go from here. I haven't seen any tracks for a while."

She could see the way he tensed and then spurred his horse toward the stream that was bubbling ahead of them. He said nothing as he dismounted, letting his horse drink, and Margaret joined him. She took in the tightness in his expression. He wiped some water over his face and cupped some in his hands, taking a drink. His face was dripping when he glanced over at her. Margaret reached into her saddle bag, which was filled with some bottled water, dried nuts, and fruit, and pulled out two granola bars. "Here," she said, reaching over Angel's saddle to extend the bar to him.

"No, you keep it." He waved it away.

"Joe, eat something. We need to stay sharp if we're going to find Ryan. If you let your blood sugar fall, it's going to slow us down."

He let out an exasperated laugh. "Always the doctor, are you?" he said. His words felt more like a sharp slap, and maybe that was mirrored on her face, because he took the bar, ripped it open, and shoved it in his mouth in two bites. "I'm not going to apologize to you every time you misread what I say, Margaret," he said, gazing across the stream and then around him. "Any idea which way to go?" he asked.

She took some comfort in what he had said, realizing she was being too sensitive. He was prickly, too, which wasn't helping the situation any. "I don't know if Ryan would cross the stream. Storm is...I never tried him around water. When you and Ryan would go out on the horses, where would you go?" she asked.

Angel finished drinking from the stream and brought her head around to Margaret, who led her over to the edge of the bank, where there were greens and small shrubs she could graze on. Joe followed.

"Haven't gone out with Ryan for a long time. It's been a few years, but I took him camping one time. We rode up on the horses to a small lake, pitched a tent, fished and spent the night. It was the same lake me and my brothers used to go to as kids." He was staring off into the hills with a wistful look.

"How many brothers do you have, again?" she asked. She remembered the Wilde brothers. The holy terrors of the county, all damn good looking, too.

"Four: Logan, Ben, Samuel, and baby Jake." He glanced back at her. "Didn't think you remembered them. Logan enlisted in the Army the day he turned eighteen. I was twelve then. That was the year you showed up here."

She flushed, because she remembered too well being dumped by her mother, who was too interested in fast-tracking her corporate career and dating her boss to take care of a daughter. Margaret wondered whether her mother knew how much she had figured out before that fateful afternoon. Her mother had come storming through the door and made Margaret pack everything she owned all because a teacher had called her at work to talk about Margaret's surly attitude and use of "the F word" in class. "I didn't exactly fit in," she said, trying to make light of her awkward years. "What about your other brothers? They were younger," she said. She needed to get the light off her, get him talking.

"Ben is one of them swanky oil execs. Jake and Samuel all took off to the big city, Seattle. Jake was always into football, and I know he was coaching for a while. Samuel is finishing up law school down in Boise. I'm pretty sure we were responsible for turning Mom gray long before her time. Man, I miss them," he said wistfully.

"I envy you," she said, and he gave her an odd look that had her stammering. "I mean, having brothers, growing up together. It was just me and Grandpa, kind of lonely."

"It wasn't always great. There wasn't enough room, with five boys bunked into a small three-bedroom house. We were crammed in pretty tight, no privacy. It led to lots of fights, bloody noses." He chirped and pulled his horse from the long grass. "Let's go. That spot I was talking about is about a three-hour ride north." He mounted his horse, and the leather of the saddle squeaked.

"Come on, Angel. Thatta girl," Margaret said. She led her horse over beside Joe and climbed up into the saddle, resting her hand on the saddle horn and taking the reins. When she looked up at Joe, he was watching her in a way that was far too familiar.

Fourteen

Every time Joe looked behind him as they wound their way deeper into the forest, Margaret was right there. Her horse picked its way through the slick, overgrown brush. The trail was starting to widen, and the trees weren't as thick. The light from the clear sky was starting to filter through.

"Ryan!" he shouted again. He kept calling every five minutes. His throat was dry, and he coughed.

"Joe, I'll call him. Give your voice a break," Margaret said. Her horse stumbled. "Easy, girl."

"You okay?" he asked, catching the way her horse tripped and then quickly righted itself.

"Joe, how close are we, do you think?" she asked, holding her reins in one hand and resting the other on her leg. Her dark slicker covered her jeans, and her hair was tucked under her wide-brimmed hat.

"Can't be much farther. I don't understand why we haven't seen any sign of him." Joe squinted and couldn't hold back his frustration. "Dammit, that kid…why?" He didn't realize he had said it out loud until Margaret came up beside him.

"Joe, don't be so hard on yourself. It won't solve anything."

"Why? You blamed me, and you were right. I asked Sara to marry me for selfish reasons. I just told myself she'd start to get used to Ryan and she just needs time to be a mother. It's new to her. I knew Ryan was frustrated, but I thought it was because of all the women I've dated." Joe didn't look at her, because all the women he'd dated and met for coffee over the past few years were starting to run together in his mind. What did that say about him?

"Wasn't there a schoolteacher in there?" she said in such a cheeky way that he realized she knew a lot more about his love life than he was comfortable with.

"Ryan told you, didn't he?"

She inclined her head and smiled. "Yeah, apparently he liked her. He told me you got scared after she spent the night."

"What?" He pulled up his horse. "Why, that little shit."

"Don't be mad at Ryan. He told me there was something like twenty women, and you had signed up for online dating. Was that how you met Sara?"

He tightened his jaw. He couldn't believe Ryan thought he had that many women walking through his door. He started to deny it, thinking back to the number of women he had been emailing in the beginning. There were a couple dozen, to the point that he had been getting confused. It had been like a drug, all those women available online, like a candy store. He had started meeting them. Some hadn't matched their profiles, listing the wrong ages. Some had been overweight, and some had been so different from their profiles that he wondered why they had bothered. Then he'd met Julie, the schoolteacher.

She was pretty, sweet, and she had liked Ryan. She had scared the crap out of him with how serious they had become. He hadn't been ready for commitment then. Margaret reminded him of Julie: smart, caring, and tall.

"Yeah, I met Sara online," he said. "She emailed me, and we met for coffee, started dating. She was the first one who made me laugh. So, what about you? Are you dating anyone?" he asked. He didn't know why, because he was pretty sure she didn't have a guy stashed off somewhere.

She shook her head and flushed, appearing to stiffen. Maybe he had hit a sore spot.

"Leave anyone behind in Seattle?" he said.

"No, I didn't leave anyone. He left me," she said. She allowed her horse to fall back, but he didn't miss the shadow of hurt that only a relationship ending badly could cause.

"I'm sorry. What happened?" he asked, glancing back. He stopped his horse until Margaret looked up at him, and the sharp brown of her eyes, which usually made him feel like she was in control, showed a self-doubt he'd never seen before.

"Keith," she said. "He was an intern, like me. I chose neurology for my residency, and he chose general surgery. We were together for two years, roommates for the last six months. He got an offer from Boston and didn't hesitate. He packed up and left, sent me a Dear Jane email. He wished me all the best, told me to have a great life." Her voice caught, and he saw her swallow hard. She forced a smile to her lips. "Ryan!" she called out.

Joe listened but heard nothing: not a horse, not a rustle, not a sound.

They rode in silence, taking turns calling out for Ryan. Margaret still couldn't believe how Joe had pulled the story of Keith out of her. It had happened right before the surgery, and she had spent days hurt over his desertion of her, as if she were nothing but someone to warm his bed at night and share the rent with. Obviously, the two years they had been together meant nothing to him. She had felt worthless, unlovable, and then her grandfather had died, all at the lowest time in her life. After the botched surgery, she had emailed Keith, believing he'd at least provide support as a friend. Instead, he had emailed back to tell her he was getting married and his fiancé wouldn't appreciate him keeping in contact with her. It had been cold, heartless, and he had seemed disinterested in her plight. That had been the final nail in her decision to hole up alone at her grandfather's.

"See that clearing up ahead? That's where the lake is, where we camped," Joe said. He started his palomino at a trot. "Ryan, where are you?" he called, but there was no answer.

They stopped in an open meadow, and a small lake stretched out before them, trees off in the distance. If this had been any other time, Margaret would have enjoyed taking a few hours to relax or pitch a tent in solitude, just sitting by the lake.

"Joe, do you see anything, any sign of him?"

"No, nothing, no tracks. I haven't see any sign they came this way." He moved his horse closer to the lake. "Dammit, where is that kid?"

"Is there another way up here, another way he would have come?" Margaret asked. She needed him to think, to relax, to keep calm, because she was freaking out, thinking the worst. Ryan was riding Storm, an excitable horse, and he was a nervous boy, running from everything. It was a bad combination that could lead to tragedy, and she didn't want to bring that up, not to Joe. God, losing a wife and then a son…what could be worse? *Stop it,* she snapped to herself. She had to stop where her thoughts were going.

"No. Shit, shit!" he shouted out in frustration. "There are a bunch of trails off here, going God knows where."

Margaret got off Angel and led her down to the lake. "We need to rest these horses a bit. Come on down, Joe. You need to eat something."

He climbed out of the saddle and let his horse drink, pulling out a rope and tying the horses so they could graze.

"Joe, we need to think about heading back," Margaret said.

He started shaking his head before she had even finished. "No, I'm not leaving until we find my son."

"Joe, we need help. This is a huge area. We need a search and rescue team. I should have thought of calling them in before we left."

"Yeah, I know, but you don't have a phone," he snapped. He pulled a cell phone from his coat pocket and held it up. "No service. There're a lot of pockets without it around here."

"Okay. Let's at least ride back far enough that you can get service. You do know where you can, right?" she asked. When she was a kid, riding the trails with her grandfather, cell phones had been big and bulky, a luxury only the wealthy had, not that there would have been service way out here, anyway.

Joe shook his head. "I don't know how far back we have to go. Here, I'll give you my cell phone. You ride back, call for help. I'll keep going."

She could see the desperation on his face, and the last thing she wanted to do was get separated. He was tired, and so was she. They'd been up all night, running on adrenaline, and the horses needed a break. "No, we'll stay together, but you need to rest first."

He started to shake his head again and took off his hat, running his fingers through his hair.

"Joe, listen." She touched his arm, which was a mistake, because just touching him had her yearning to throw her arms around him and hug him, wishing he'd pull her into his arms and hold her, too. She wanted it so badly. "The horses will be no good to us unless we give them a break. We've been on the move since last night."

Joe's deep blue eyes were gritty and bloodshot, just like her own. Now that they had stopped, she wanted to rest, and her head was feeling heavy. Even just an hour would help. She reached behind her saddle and unwrapped the mat and bedroll, setting it on the ground, in a dry spot under the trees. When she glanced back at Joe and saw his worry and stress, she realized she'd made the right choice. Whatever happened, she couldn't leave him alone.

CHAPTER
Fifteen

Joe stared out at the miles of vast wilderness. This was just one of many hidden pockets, and he wondered whether Ryan would have thought to come way up here. They could be off, way off. After all, he'd had a hard time finding the path in the dark when he started out with Margaret in the rain. What had Ryan been thinking, heading out on Storm into this? Ryan had never ridden alone. Joe would never have allowed it.

A hand touched his arm, and then Margaret stood right beside him with that ridiculous wide-brimmed hat that wasn't made for a woman. She watched him, standing so close that he could feel her support, which was something he'd never felt from a woman before. He'd always been the support, the strong one, the one to hold everything together, and he liked that, but he found Margaret comforting at times, and he really liked being with her.

"I'm glad you're here. Thanks for coming with me," he said. He looked away when he saw her discomfort. Damn, the woman couldn't handle a compliment.

"Of course," she said. "Don't thank me, though. I'm

pretty sure I didn't give you much of a choice. I care so much about Ryan. He's such a great kid."

There was something in her expression when she spoke about Ryan that he had never seen on one of his girl-friends' faces—certainly never on Sara's. Sara tolerated Ryan. She was polite, and so was he, but Ryan always left the room when Sara was around, and she never encouraged him to stay. With Margaret, well, wasn't it just about Storm? Now he wondered. What else had he missed with his son?

"I didn't realize you and Ryan were getting so close," he said.

She had such a vibrancy, a life, that it shone from her eyes when something she was talking about filled her with passion. "Ryan feels comfortable talking to me," she said. "He's a great kid, but he holds on to so much. I guess I recognized myself in him, you know, two peas in a pod." She touched his arm again. "Come and sit down over here. Rest for a bit." She reached for something in the saddle bag, pulling out a water bottle and a bag of nuts. Then she started walking to where she had set the bedroll in the driest spot under the trees.

Joe followed. "So what has Ryan been telling you?" he asked. For some reason, hearing that his kid felt more comfortable talking with someone else made him feel inadequate, as if he was a bad parent. "Is there a problem? Is he keeping secrets from me? Did he say he was going to take off?" He was starting to get himself worked up as he followed her to where she sat cross-legged and patted a spot for him to sit beside her.

"Come on, Joe. Sit down." She unscrewed the lid to a water bottle and held it out to him. "Drink. You have to have some water."

Joe hesitated and then took the water bottle, taking a

drink and then handing it back to Margaret. She didn't bother to wipe the rim before taking a swallow. He sat beside her on the ground, feeling her heat and taking in her long legs as she extended them in front of her. Joe crossed his legs beside her and leaned back against the tree, his shoulder bumping hers. She opened the bag of nuts and offered him a handful, shaking it a bit when he didn't shove his hand in right away.

"Thanks," he said. He was touched by her generosity, such a simple thing that someone did when they cared. He didn't remember a time when a woman had put his interests and comforts first—other than Evie.

"Ryan never felt threatened by me," she said. "I don't know what it was, but from day one, he started sharing little bits about himself, just like Storm did. They each had their own story to tell. When we own a horse, we have to become really comfortable with ourselves, to learn the horses' language, the way they speak. Horses are honest, and they'll always tell you the truth. I guess I just allowed Ryan to do the same thing."

"So Ryan told you what an awful person I am," he said. He couldn't help it. He was worried his kid had said something bad about him. "Ryan should have come to me about his problems."

She touched his hand, and he took in her long, slender fingers. She had short, clipped nails, efficient, different from the long, painted nails Sara wore. He turned his hand over, and she linked her fingers with his, squeezing gently.

"Ryan loves you very much," she said, "but there are times when we feel misunderstood, and talking to someone who understands is the only thing that helps. I was just an ear for Ryan. He feels you're disappointed in him, and Storm picked up on his fear of all his failings."

"He said that?"

"No, not in so many words. This is about what he didn't say, too." She chewed on some nuts, and he wondered, by the way she was watching, whether she was judging him.

"Then what did he say, in so many words? Did he tell you he was going to take off?" he said. She flinched, because it came out much harsher than he expected. "Sorry."

"Look, Joe, I know you're upset. Ryan didn't say he was going to run off. He was shocked when you announced you were going to marry Sara. He felt betrayed. I saw it. I know you couldn't. You made him get in the truck with you when he wanted to do some work with Storm. He feels you don't hear him, and even though you told me you were marrying Sara to give him a mother…" She stopped and shook her head. "Joe, you want Sara for you. Be honest, at least, about that. Sara isn't interested in Ryan. Ask yourself, when has she ever had a real conversation with him, or tried to make him feel comfortable, or made any effort to spend time with him or get to know him?"

"She just needs time, and so does he, to get to know each other," he said, realizing it didn't sound true even to his own ears.

"Joe, seriously, you can't make someone be comfortable with your kid. Maybe down the road, they'll tolerate each other, but in case you didn't notice, neither gives the other a second glance when they're together. They avoid each other. Sara looks anywhere where he isn't, as if she truly doesn't see him. Ryan knows, and it hurts him. Why do you think he was pushing so hard to have me around, begging me to come to his party, making me believe that you wanted me there? I figured it out. In case you didn't notice, it was me he ran to, not Sara." She chewed on some nuts and looked out at the lake.

"Why are you so comfortable with my son?" he asked.

She hesitated and stopped chewing for a minute, looking down at her lap, their fingers still linked. She pulled her hand away about the same time he could feel something about her pulling in. "I really like him. Other than the fact that he reminds me of myself, he's such an amazing kid, Joe. Deep down, he really wants to please you. I understand what he's doing. I understand the feeling of not being wanted."

"Why the hell would you say that? He's my kid—don't ever say I don't want him!" He was on his feet, fisting his hands.

She stood up and stepped right into his space, meeting his gaze and stepping closer. This woman wasn't afraid of him at all. "That's not what I meant, Joe. I know you love him. I can see that. With that horse alone, you push him because you love him, but sometimes, when we push too hard and do what we believe is best, things actually backfire. He won't say anything to you because he doesn't think you'll listen. With Sara and the other women you dated, he always made fun of that until you started getting serious. No matter what you do or did, he doesn't like Sara because she doesn't accept him. He feels you chose her over him, and he can't tell you. He'd rather get himself killed by Storm than say one word to you about how he's really feeling!" she said. Joe began to speak, but she cut him off.

"Storm is an excitable, high-energy horse, and he needs someone to match his energy. The emotion between you and Ryan…of course the horse is picking it up! If you start looking back on when you started having problems with Storm, you'd see the change that happened in your life. Ryan wasn't as secure, he was uncertain, he was stressed. Every second of his life went into that ring with him, and Storm felt it. Ryan's not that confident. He needs a horse who's quieter, slower, older, more stable. He can start at the beginning. He needs to know you hear him, and you have to pay attention to him, because he says so much, Joe, without uttering one word."

Her face lit up when she talked about his son, and if he'd ever had any doubt about how much she cared about Ryan, he didn't anymore. "You love him, don't you?" Joe said.

She blushed and set both hands over her cheeks. "How could I not?"

Joe placed his hands over hers. He lowered his gaze to her nose, narrow and long, and to her full, pink lips, wondering whether she had ever worn any color but her own. She had light brown freckles over the bridge of her nose and a soft chin that hardened when she was tense. Her eyes were big, full, brown, unable to hide any of the passion, pain, and heartache she had. She was such a passionate, honest woman, and he didn't know why he hadn't allowed himself to see it before now. When her eyes drifted to his lips and he felt her breathing become heavier, he couldn't help himself from leaning in, setting his lips to hers gently, softly. He pulled away a fraction, feeling her warm breath. With no hesitation, he deepened the kiss, angling his mouth to hers, tasting her, his tongue touching hers. Her hat was gone, and his was on the ground, too, as he reached into her long, dark hair and ran his fingers through it.

Her hands slid up his back, her arms around him, and he set his hand behind her head, holding her to him as he slid his other down over her buttocks, pulling her to him. She stepped closer, pressing her curves into him, her fingers working into his shoulders, his back, as if she couldn't get closer. He held her tight against him as he lifted her, and then they were on the ground. He pressed her arms above her head, and she hooked her long legs around his hips. He kissed her as if she were his last breath. He reached down and ripped open the snaps of her coat, lifting her sweater and bra and taking her breast, first one nipple and then the other, in his mouth, sucking and watching as her body lifted to him, closer.

She gasped and called out his name: "Joe, oh my God, Joe!" She had her hands under his coat, opening the snaps and then going for his belt buckle at the same time he ripped open hers. He pulled back just a few seconds to pull down her jeans as she toed off a boot and got one pant leg off. He unzipped and didn't wait or be sure she was ready as he pushed into her hard and fast, and she locked her legs around his. He took her hands again and pressed them above her head, watching her as he moved.

Her eyes showed every emotion she was feeling, and he could see the moment he stripped her down that her heart had cracked open and he could step in. She was bare, innocent, and he realized he could probably get her to do anything. He could see how badly she would hurt and bleed, and he still couldn't stop. He had to have her. This need, it was like the way a junkie needed crack. "Margaret, you feel so good," he said.

She whimpered beneath him, and he felt her tighten around him as he let himself go.

Margaret's heart was racing as Joe collapsed, all his weight on top of her. His heart was pounding to the same beat as hers. She ran her hand under his shirt, feeling his warm, bare skin and the muscles in his back. He was still inside her, and she felt wet and wonderful, but then she remembered Ryan, and Sara, and she started to push at his chest. "Get off," she said.

"What the hell?" he muttered.

He pulled out of her, and she scrambled to her feet, her jeans bunched around one ankle. She turned her back to him. She couldn't look at him, because she was suddenly embarrassed for throwing herself at him. Just who had kissed who first? She couldn't remember. Her hands were shaking as she stepped into her jeans, stepping a sock foot on the wet ground. Every moment, she could hear Joe behind her, standing up, zipping up his pants, letting out a sigh of irritation, annoyance—hell, she didn't know what it was. She heard the clink of his belt buckle, and she shut her eyes again as she zipped up her pants, pulled down her bra and sweater, and snapped up her coat. She turned, keeping her eyes to the ground as she searched out her boot, which was scattered out a ways. When Joe reached for it and then stepped into her line of sight, she did everything to look away until he took her jaw and leaned into her face.

"I'm sorry, but you didn't act like you didn't want to be fucked," he said.

Her mouth gaped at his crudeness, and she stumbled back as if he had slapped her. "Is that all I am to you, someone to satisfy you? Well, you've had your fun. I have to tell you, I'm not a one-night stand. I'm not made that way. The casual sex that you men get off on is not something I can do." She started to say she wanted him to make love to her, that she had dreamed of it, but not like this. The words froze on her tongue. She couldn't shake the sense of being back in that same, dark place as the unlovable woman Keith had left. She was doomed to repeat the cycle again and again. He hadn't been as careful as Keith, and he'd left part of himself inside her. Maybe this was her one chance at having someone to love. She lowered her hand to her abdomen and set it there for a minute before glancing up at Joe. The man's face was torn and weary, on the edge of breaking.

He handed her the boot, and she took it and pulled it on. "We should start riding before we lose light," he said.

She didn't say a word as she bent down, shaking off the leaves and pine needles and dirt from the bedroll before rolling it up. She didn't look up as she heard him turn and walk away.

He rode with Margaret behind him in silence for hours, each one taking turns calling out for Ryan, Joe checking his cell phone over and over as they took one trail after another, weaving their way further away from home. The atmosphere was tense. He'd hurt her badly. He knew it, and if it wasn't for the fact that he was worried sick about his son, he'd have tried to talk to her, to smooth it over. He was confused as all hell about his feelings for Margaret and for Sara. He seemed to be screwing up one thing after the other, starting from what he had done to Evie. He wondered whether he could do anything right.

He heard something, a whinny, and stopped, holding his hand out to Margaret. "Did you hear that?" he said. He glanced back at her and the shadows of the forest around her as they listened. "Ryan!" he shouted again.

Margaret looked around and then called out, "Storm, here boy!" She whistled and chirped, urging her horse forward and cutting through the brush heading down the hill where they had heard the horse.

"Be careful," Joe said behind her, but nothing was

holding her back as she moved through the forest, zigzagging through the trees. Her horse stumbled once, and then Joe saw Storm, still saddled, his reins dangling on the ground. He appeared to be trembling, his eyes wild. Margaret stopped Angel and climbed out of the saddle calmly.

"Stay back, Joe," she ordered, tossing her reins to him. "Let me get him."

Joe grabbed her hand, because he took one look at that horse and knew this was an accident waiting to happen. He wished he'd brought his gun. "Just be careful," he said.

She nodded. "Joe, let go. I'll be careful, but I have to see if he's hurt. I know what I'm doing."

He eased his grip, and she slipped away, holding out her hands as she stepped carefully toward the horse. "Whoa, easy there, Storm. That's a good boy," she said. She kept her voice calm and reassuring, but he wasn't taking his eyes off her. If that horse did anything to hurt Margaret, he'd be in there, and he was ready with his palomino, keeping it steady and holding Angel's reins beside him.

Storm snorted and reared up, screaming out before stomping to the ground, pawing and sidestepping. Margaret kept going slowly, walking as if she meant every step, setting all her focus on the horse. Joe wanted to yell at her to get back when she reached for the reins and then touched Storm's neck. The horse was wild and out of control, rolling the whites of his eyes, his head high and frantic.

"Whoa, easy there," she said over and over.

As he watched, there was something magical about her. She appeared to draw the horse in, to offer him relief. Joe watched, paying attention to what she was doing for the first time. He'd never seen her this way. He'd also never taken the time to stay when she was with Ryan, and he realized now that there were so many things he wanted to say to his son. He hoped and prayed he'd have the chance. This woman had reached his son when he couldn't, just like this beast that he had been so quick to write off. She was calming him and moving him, and the horse started to respond a bit. She kept moving his back end, pulling and releasing, and the horse began to respond to her.

"Joe, the stirrup is broken," she said. "There's brush stuck in the side of his saddle. He could have been running a long way. He's got a gash on his side, too. It's not bad, but…"

The horse was a mess, with mud coating the back of his legs, his hocks, his back end. Joe climbed down from the saddle and started toward Margaret, but Storm reacted and reared up, screaming.

"Joe, stay there," she said. She raised her hands and calmed Storm again, but he was having none of it.

"Any sign of Ryan?" Joe called out.

Storm lowered his head a bit, and she patted his neck. "Good boy. There, it's okay. No one is going to hurt you," she murmured. "No, Joe, there's no sign of him here. There's a rope in my saddle bag. I need it. Can you walk over with it very slowly and calmly?"

Joe did as she said, glancing over at the way she started to move Storm and then walked him over to where he was rummaging in the saddle bag as he held the reins for both horses. He pulled it out and handed it to her, and she didn't give Storm a chance to freak out, as she moved him backwards and then to the side, getting him to think. Joe knew that if a horse was working, having to think, it wouldn't spook. This horse needed more than he could give, more than Ryan could give, but not Margaret. This was easy for her.

She looped the rope around the ring of his halter, which Ryan had obviously put on him under the bridle, and then she tied it loosely to a tree, letting him graze. "Joe, if we can figure out the direction he came from, we can backtrack."

He started down the trail until he found a fork. "We can't take him," Joe barked, heading back to Mercedes.

"I'll take him behind Angel. We can't leave him. He wouldn't make it," she said. She waited until Joe mounted his horse. "Start down the trail. I'll be right behind you."

Joe hesitated when she took the reins from him and walked over to Storm, and he watched as she untied him and held the rope while she mounted Angel. Storm decided to spook and sidestep, but Margaret spoke softly and moved a step . She didn't face Joe when she said, "Joe, start down the trail. He's scared, and we need to move."

He knew they did. The shadows around them were growing darker, and they were losing light fast. He looked to the ground, searching for tracks, spotting prints in the mud left from Storm's shoes. He was glad he'd had him shoed, now, as it was making his son easier to track. He glanced back and saw Margaret talking the horse down, and he kept looking back. "Are you okay?"

"Keep going, Joe," she replied. "We're fine."

Joe kicked Mercedes. "Come on, let's go." He spotted a steep hill bearing tracks that let him know Storm had raced up it, and that was when he spotted a red backpack that looked far too much like Ryan's.

"Ryan!" he shouted. He vaguely heard Storm squeal behind him and Margaret trying to calm him.

"Joe, what's wrong?" she called out as he leaped out of his saddle and skidded down in the mud to the backpack.

"It's Ryan's!" he said.

"Is he there?"

He was frantic as he slipped down. The backpack was torn, and one of the straps was broken. "Ryan, where are you? Answer me, son!" he cried. He listened, and all he could hear was a rustling behind him as Margaret slipped down. He looked around when she slid into him.

She touched him and then grabbed his shoulder. "Joe," she said frantically, and her breath went out of her in a way that turned his blood to ice. She moved away, skidding on her knees, stumbling over a log. For a minute, everything went into slow motion as he turned and blinked, and Margaret was running, batting away the brush, the branches and leaves, yelling something he couldn't register as she sank to her knees over Ryan's still form.

Margaret's hand shook as she touched Ryan. He was cold and still, with a gash at his hairline, his dark hair matted with blood.

"Margaret!" Joe was frantic, skidding beside her and moving to scoop Ryan up.

"Don't touch him!" she yelled, reaching for Joe's arm and holding it. She pressed her fingers to the pulse point at Ryan's neck and lowered her ear to his chest, listening for his breathing.

"Margaret, is he alive? Margaret!" Joe was yelling, and she slowly sat up and shook her head.

"His pulse is weak," she said. She struggled to remember her training, and for a minute, the face of the boy lying there changed to a boy she knew as Charlie. It was amazing, the details that came to her in a moment like this as she noticed the dried blood splattered across his face, his pale skin that was cool to the touch. She shrugged out of her coat and laid it over him. Joe's hand was shaking as he touched his son's head, tears glistening in his eyes.

"Joe, I need your help," she said. "He's hypothermic.

Go up to the horses and bring down the blanket and tarp, the water. There's a first aid kit in the pouch, as well. Bring it all down."

"You keep my boy alive," he said, and Margaret couldn't help reliving the fear of that father's vengeance, when she had to tell him what she'd done to his son, how she'd screwed up.

"Go, Joe! Can you get any cell service?"

He stood up and checked his phone. "One bar."

"Call for help now, and then get everything."

He was on the phone, and she watched him as he stood and frantically ran his hands over his head, knocking his hat off, yelling at whomever he was talking to when he couldn't give the exact location.

He turned to her. "They said to leave my phone on, and they're sending help." He pulled off his coat and handed it to her, and she set it over Ryan. Joe slipped and crawled through the mud up the hill to the horses, and she vaguely heard Storm's snort. Then Joe was coming back down, his arms full with her bedroll, a tarp, her saddle bag. He dumped everything beside him and handed her the first aid kit.

Margaret could feel her hands sweating even though she was far from warm, and she hesitated as she watched Ryan, a boy she loved, lying so still, barely breathing. For the first time, she truly understood how Charlie's father could hate her so much.

———

Watching his son lying helpless and bleeding and barely alive, Joe silently prayed. *Please, Evie, don't take him,* he thought. *Please, I won't screw up again.*

Margaret was yelling at him now, her hand shaking.

"Joe, I need your help!" She had scissors and was cutting Ryan's sweatshirt open. He was fighting for shallow breaths, but his eyes were still closed. "Light, I need the flashlight! We're losing light fast."

It was in the pile beside him with the tarp and a backpack. He grabbed everything and flicked it on just as Margaret exposed Ryan's bare chest and pressed her ear to it. His chest was discolored.

"Margaret, what is it?"

She raised her head, and he'd never seen her look so helpless. "I think he busted a couple ribs and punctured a lung."

"What does that mean?"

She just looked down at Ryan and then shut her eyes. He wanted to reach across and shake her. "It means he's not getting the oxygen he needs," she said.

"You mean he's drowning in his own blood. Margaret, could he die?" he cried. He watched as she sat back and raised her knee, resting her hand on it and looking down as if she didn't know what to do. "Margaret!" he yelled, and she looked up at him with tears in her eyes.

"Yes," she said.

He reached over his boy and grabbed her. "You're not going to let him die. You're a surgeon! You know what to do."

"Yes, in an emergency room, with equipment, and a sterile environment, and an operating table…" Her voice caught as she whispered the last part.

"You don't have an emergency room. You can handle any challenge—you know that. You can do anything you set your mind to. What do you need?"

"I need a syringe, two, preferably, and a gauge, and…"

"No, Margaret, look at what we've got. Come on, think. What can we use here?"

She shook her hands, and Joe let her go as she grabbed the first aid kit and rummaged through it, first grabbing the pen light and clicking it on. She leaned forward and opened Ryan's eyes, shining the light in one and then the other. She dropped the light into the pack and grabbed a packet, handing it to Joe. "It's an alcohol wipe. Tear it open for me."

He ripped it open, and she gestured to Ryan's chest. "Wipe it," she said. She pressed her fingers to his chest and lowered her head again, shutting her eyes and listening. When she looked up at Joe, she cried out, "Joe, God help me! I don't want to screw up again, not with Ryan."

He reached for her arm. "You won't screw up. You listen to me. You're good, and you can do anything. You know what to do. Trust that." He willed her to believe in herself, because this wasn't the time for her to have any doubts. She slowly nodded, picking up a needle from her field medical kit. With shaking hands, she felt her way over Ryan's chest.

"Joe, I need light. Shine it over his chest. I need to see. I need to insert this needle, not too far, just enough to relieve the pressure. There's blood pooling in his lung, and he can't breathe."

"You can do this," he said, holding her gaze and willing her to be strong.

As he silently prayed, she injected the needle. His son gasped, and lights shone above them from a chopper, blades whirring through the air overhead.

Nineteen

"You've got a lucky boy. Someone knew how to keep him alive," the doctor said. He had gray hair and appeared close to retirement, wearing faded green scrubs and standing on the other side of Ryan's hospital bed. He scribbled something in a chart and then glanced down at Ryan, frowning. "That was a very stupid thing to do, young man, scaring your parents like that, running off on a horse. You're lucky they found you."

Ryan's head was wrapped in bandages. He had thirty-six stitches across his hairline, a gash on the back of his head, and a concussion, though only one broken rib that had punctured his lung.

The doctor looked over at Joe. "You should go home and get some sleep. Your boy's going to be fine," he said.

The fact was that Joe didn't think he could leave Ryan's side again. He'd never felt the kind of fear he had when he saw Ryan lying bloody and helpless in the mud. Joe and Ryan had been airlifted out, and Margaret had stayed with the horses, telling him she'd be fine and she needed to get them home. He hadn't thought twice about her until the doctor stepped out of surgery and said it had gone well. Ryan opened his eyes a few hours later, and then Joe started to worry.

A soft hand touched his arm, and he smelled her before she said anything. She slid her arm around his waist, sliding up against him, setting her hand on his chest. "I was so worried about you when you didn't call," Sara said. "And you, scaring your dad like that, how could you?"

Ryan just shut his eyes and turned his head away.

The doctor glanced down at him, flipped the chart closed, and said, "He needs some sleep. Don't stay too long."

Joe watched the doctor leave, and Sara looked up at him with such worry. "Joe, you look so tired. You need to get some sleep. After you're rested, you can come back and see Ryan." She didn't glance Ryan's way, and this time, when Joe looked back over at Ryan, he could see what Margaret had been saying—well, some of it.

"Ryan," he said, touching his arm and leaning over, "I'll be right back."

"Dad, was the doctor talking about Margaret? Was it Margaret who helped me, or did I dream it?" Ryan asked. His voice was so raspy, and Joe could tell it hurt for him to talk.

"Save your voice. Margaret went with me to find you. If it wasn't for her…" He stopped and shook his head, because he didn't want to go there, even though the grave of his son had flashed before him when he kneeled beside Margaret.

"And Storm?" Ryan choked out.

He was even worried about the damn horse. "Margaret found him. She's bringing him back," Joe said. With the horses and everything, she had about a day's ride alone.

His son's eyes widened. "Is she…" he started to ask, but Joe touched his arm.

"No more talking," he said. The fact was that Joe needed to find out where she was, whether she had made it back. Since Ryan was stable, he could step out long enough to call her, talk to her, and thank her. Then he remembered she had no phone. "Go to sleep now, Ryan," he said.

There was something sad in his son's expression when he glanced at Sara, who was still attached to Joe, as if she belonged there, that made Joe's mouth harden. He had gotten the message loud and clear. He set his arm around Sara and said, "Come on, let's go," and guided her from the room.

"Joe, let's go home" she said. "I'll get you settled, make some dinner. You can get some sleep…"

"No, I can't, Sara. I can't leave here." He took both her hands in his. "You don't deserve this."

"What are you talking about?" she asked.

"I asked you to marry me because I wanted a mother for Ryan. He needs guidance, and I thought a woman's influence was needed." He watched as she blinked a couple times and realized she always wore makeup, not heavy, but shadow, mascara, even lipstick that matched her painted nails. Her hair was always curled, and she always smelled like the floral perfume she wore. Margaret wasn't like that. She sweated and didn't care or try to hide it.

"Well, of course," Sara said. "I won't tolerate this kind of thing from Ryan. When we're married, you'll just have to get rid of the horse."

Joe let out a laugh, but it was more of disbelief than anything else. He crossed his arms. "Are you kidding? Ryan taking off wasn't because of the horse or any horse problem. It was because of what I did, asking you to marry me. Apparently, he believes you don't like him."

Her jaw slackened. "That's not true, Joe, and that's not fair. I'm not a monster. I love you, and I realize Ryan and you are a package deal."

He waited for her to say she cared about Ryan, but nothing came.

"Sara, this is a mistake. I don't love you," he said, watching as tears popped into her eyes.

"What?" She stepped back, holding both her hands up.

"Sara, I'm sorry. I didn't mean to hurt you, but Ryan means more to me than anything."

She started to step away, but she turned back and slapped Joe across the face. It stung, and when she went to slap him again, he grabbed her wrist. "You hit me once, and I deserved that," he said.

She pulled her hand away. "This is about that frumpy horse woman, isn't it? I've seen the way you look at her, the way you drool over her. You're interested. I'm not stupid."

When Joe went to deny it, she stepped back, shaking her head. "I'm not an idiot, Joe, so don't treat me like one," she said. Then she turned and left, bumping into a tall, dark-haired man who gripped her shoulders and said, "Whoa, there. You okay, ma'am?"

"Fine, I'm sorry," she snapped, turning and hurrying away as Joe looked over at his big brother, Logan. The man was six foot three, with cropped hair tinged gray at the sides. Logan narrowed his eyes at Sara's dramatic exit and looked back to Joe.

"That's a nice handprint on your face, there, little brother," he said.

Joe paused only a second before crossing the distance, and Logan set his hands on Joe's shoulders, pulling him close and hugging him.

CHAPTER

Twenty

Margaret had worried herself sick, watching as the helicopter airlifted Ryan away. Even though she had relieved the pressure and he could breathe, there were a whole host of things that could still go wrong, with a possible infection, not to mention how bad his head injury was.

Joe had been frantic, but when Search and Rescue sent down a stretcher, he had gone up with his son only after Margaret insisted. Of course he had to go with Ryan—he would have worried himself to death otherwise. Margaret had been too numb to think clearly when the volunteer asked if she was okay getting back. She'd nodded, saying she had to take the horses. She'd be fine. The fact was that she was far from fine, and when the helicopter lifted off, her shaking legs had finally given out, and she'd dropped down on her knees and cried. Only after the chopper left and she heard the frantic spooking of the horses, neighing and rustling around, did she realize the enormity of the situation and how terrified the horses were.

She glanced at the mess: the tarps, the blankets, her

first aid kit, hers and Joe's coats, and blood everywhere. She started cleaning up and packing everything so she could carry it up and load it on the backs of the horses. Of course, she needed the flashlight to go up the hill, as the darkness started settling around them. Angel and Mercedes were exactly where she had tied them, and Storm was side-stepping and spooking still from the excitement of the helicopter hovering above. She was surprised the horses were still here, but she'd tied Storm well to a sturdy tree branch. She ended up tying what she could on Mercedes and had to take a minute to calm herself before figuring out the best way to take all the horses back. On top of that, she still had to remember the route home. She'd never been out this way before, and now, as she stood in the middle of the darkened wilderness, alone, she wished Joe had stayed. For the first time, she didn't want to be alone.

Margaret didn't make it very far on Angel, leading Mercedes and Storm behind her, before she was forced to stop until there was enough light for her to see. With the bedroll and tarp, she tried to rest under a large fir tree, the only shelter she could find. The rain started about an hour later. It was miserable and cold, and she was wet and hungry and scared as she listened to the night sounds of the suddenly unfriendly forest.

At the first sliver of light, her head pounding from lack of sleep, her hands shaking, she rode out, leading the horses until they stopped at another fork, where she tried to remember which trail to take. "Well, if I had a coin, I suppose I could flip it. Come on, Angel. Tell me, girl, which way?"

Margaret loosened the reins and let her horse choose, praying she did, in fact, know the way home.

Logan stepped away, and Joe was embarrassed for a minute that his brother had seen Sara try to emasculate him. "What are you doing here, anyway?" he asked.

"I called your place, and some woman answered, said Ryan took off and you'd gone after him," Logan said. "I was going to drop in and see you two. I was visiting Mom and Dad in Boise, and I thought they didn't need to hear you were having trouble, so I came myself. I ran into Stan Jerow—doesn't look as if he's aged a day, still bald. He waved me down, said Ryan had been airlifted to the hospital, hurt bad by some runaway horse."

Joe wondered if half the town had heard that story. Sometimes, Stan and Hazel could do more damage with their mouths and their gossip than anything else.

"That's not entirely true," Joe said. He started over to the window of the waiting area as some people wandered in. His brother followed his gaze, taking in what he was wearing. Since he hadn't changed, he realized he must look pretty bad, as his brother made a face at his jeans, now covered in dried mud. His shirt was also filthy, and he even felt the grime on his face and in his hair. "Ryan ran away and took the horse, Storm, who he shouldn't have been riding. I had a…" He stopped, because he didn't know how to describe Margaret—as a friend, as someone he had shagged, as someone he had left to bring the horses in alone? He had talked her into working with Storm in the first place, and he still needed to find out how she was. Logan was watching him with an odd look.

"You had a what?" he asked.

"A friend went with me to find him. He was thrown, hurt bad. She saved him, and he was airlifted out. Because of her, he's going to be fine, but if she hadn't been there, he wouldn't have made it. He has a punctured lung, a broken rib, some gashes in his head, and only a concussion. He's lucky. I'm lucky. I left her out there to bring the horses in herself, and I was on the chopper with Ryan. I haven't even called to see if Search and Rescue sent anyone in to help her. I don't even know if she knows the way back." He ran his hand roughly over his face. "What kind of man does that to a woman?"

"So who's the woman who hit you?" Logan said, gesturing to the hallway where Sara had gone. "I take it that's not the one who went with you to find Ryan, and who was the woman who answered your phone?"

If Joe wasn't so tired, he'd probably have felt embarrassed about the mess, because the way his brother said it made him sound like one of those lowlife womanizers who used women and tossed them aside. He never did that, except he could still vividly remember taking Margaret on the ground while he was engaged to another woman.

"That was Sara. She was my fiancé and the reason Ryan ran away."

His brother raised his eyebrows but didn't say a word.

"Margaret Gordon, I don't know if you remember

her," Joe said. "She's my age, a tall girl who moved in with her grandfather, Carl Spick."

"Oh, I remember Carl. Yeah, that tall girl dumped here by a mother who had no time for her. I remember Mom talking," Logan said.

"She's back, and she works with horses. She was working with Storm, and Ryan likes her. She befriended him. She went with me to find him, and she saved him. It's a long story, but she used to be a doctor. She knew the entire time that Ryan and Sara didn't get along. Ryan doesn't like Sara, and I was apparently not seeing the whole picture. I only asked Sara to marry me because I thought Ryan needed a mother." He rubbed his cheek. "I deserved this."

"Hmm" was all his brother said, studying him shrewdly. There was one thing about Logan: He'd grown quieter since becoming a marine. His brother limped over to a chair and sat down.

"Your leg still bothering you?" Joe said. He remembered all too well the roadside bomb that had left Logan in a coma, without his spleen, with internal injuries, his leg pieced back together. He had been medically discharged shortly afterward.

"It's the wet, and I've been driving all day," Logan said. He winced and stretched out his leg. "It sounds like you've got bigger problems. At least you came to your senses before you married the woman. You did, didn't you?"

Joe wiped his face with his hands. "Yeah. Listen, I need to find out if Margaret made it back. I'm worried about her. I haven't told Ryan yet, but he's asked about her. I don't want to leave him."

Logan groaned as he shoved his way out of his seat. "Stay with Ryan. I'll go find this Gordon woman."

"Thank you, Logan," Joe said. "Oh, she doesn't have a

phone. We took the trail from Carl's, the one that headed up to that lake where we always went to camp."

"You took her all the way up there?" Logan said, shaking his head. "I'll stop at her house first. You only had the two horses, didn't you?"

"No, I have a silver dapple, but she can't wear a saddle," Joe said, worrying as his brother tried to hide the pain in his leg.

"I guess I'll be walking, then."

Joe couldn't help it when he glanced at Logan's leg and said, "Are you sure you're up to it?"

The stubborn, hard expression that Logan was known for, which had gotten him in trouble time and again, darkened his face. "I'm up to a hell of a lot more than you are," he replied. "Go look after your son."

Joe watched as his brother strode out, trying to hide the fact that his leg was the one thing that would hold him back from being a hero.

Twenty~Two

Margaret wondered if she was lost. She did her best to look for anything familiar, but the trees, the paths, the brown and green, everything looked the same. She wondered if Angel was just taking her on a wild goose chase. She was so tired that she didn't have her wits about her. Storm had tested her over and over, spooking at everything, and Margaret just wasn't in the frame of mind to easily calm him. Everything was an effort. Her shoulders ached from riding for hours. Her hand and arm hurt so badly from leading both Mercedes and Storm, and her right shoulder felt as if she'd jarred it. Her neck was twisted into knots, and her head was pounding. Tears leaked from the corners of her eyes. Maybe that was why Storm suddenly spooked and pulled so hard he yanked her off Angel. She hit the ground at the same time that she heard a man yell, and her breath went out in a whoosh. She didn't think, rolling to avoid being stomped. She saw stars as she struggled to her feet, reaching for Angel, who was still there. She blinked when a man who looked so much like Joe appeared, grabbing Mercedes.

"Joe?" she said, shaking her head when she noticed the short hair, the gray, the lines on his face.

"You must be Margaret. I'm Logan, Joe's brother. Are you okay?"

"Yeah, fine," she said before she had a chance to think about it.

The man reached forward and touched her forehead. "You have a cut. It's bleeding a bit."

Margaret touched her forehead and pulled her hand away, seeing blood, but she couldn't feel anything. Adrenaline was still pulsing through her, and she was so tired. When she took a step and winced from the pain in her leg, and then her shoulder, she cried out.

"Joe was worried about you," Logan said, and Margaret rested her hand on Angel's flank.

"How is Ryan? Is he okay?" she said. The fact was that she'd been sick with worry and didn't know whether she could handle it if something had happened to Ryan.

"He's going to be okay. Apparently you're the one to thank for that. You saved his life," Logan said.

"What about a CT scan, did they do one? Does he have a head injury? He had a punctured lung—what about other internal injuries?" she said. She was still rattling on when he set his hand on her shoulder.

"Well, I'll tell you what: As soon as we get back, I'll take you to see him, and you can see for yourself that he's all right."

"And Joe, is he okay?" she said.

Logan seemed a little amused. "Joe's fine, but I think he was right to be worried about you. I can't believe he left you out here alone," he added.

"He didn't have a choice. He had to go with Ryan, and I couldn't leave the horses." Her legs were starting to shake. "Would you mind giving me a leg up? I don't think I have the strength."

Logan did more than give her a leg up. He slid his arm around her to steady her and all but lifted her into the saddle, handing her the reins.

Margaret looked back for Storm. "Storm, come here, boy."

"I'll get him," Logan said, taking Mercedes' reins and pulling himself into the saddle.

"Storm spooks really easily, Logan. Let me get him," Margaret said.

Logan moved beside her, setting his hand on her arm. "You've done more than enough. I'll get Storm, and…"

"You don't understand. Storm is—"

He stopped her by gripping her wrist. "I've got it. I've handled a lot worse."

There was something about the way he said it that had her nodding and focusing on staying in the saddle with Angel. She thought she could easily fall over and onto the ground, and she listened to Storm squealing. From the tone of Logan's voice, she knew the moment he had him, and then he was beside her.

"Are you ready to go home?" he asked.

"How much farther is it?"

He gave her an odd look. "You were almost home, just through those trees up ahead." He kicked the palomino and moved forward, holding the rope tied to Storm and leading the way.

Margaret was never so grateful to see home as when she spotted the corral, the barn, and the house. She saw an older model black Jeep, which she supposed was Logan's. She stopped in a daze and just sat in the saddle outside the small barn, and the next she knew, Logan had lifted her out of the saddle and set her on the ground. She would have fallen over if he hadn't been holding her.

"You okay?" he asked.

"I'm just tired—and sore," she said, and he finally loosened his hold. "I need to get the horses put away. They need to be unsaddled and given some hay, water. This has been a hard couple of days for them. I need to get them brushed down, and…" She wiped her arm across her forehead, rubbing at the dried blood that was starting to itch.

"Listen, I'll take care of the horses," Logan said. "You need some rest. Are you sure you're not hurt? That was a hard fall you took."

As he let her go, she swayed a bit and then stepped away, limping. Her entire body felt like one big bruise. "Nothing a hot shower won't help," she said.

She watched as he led Angel beside the other two horses. He tied them to the post of the corral and then unsaddled her, taking the blanket and all to the barn and shouting over his shoulder, "Go, get in the shower. I told you I'll look after them."

It was then she noticed the limp in his leg and realized he was the eldest of the Wildes, the one who had fought in the war. She took comfort in knowing someone was looking out for her, and she went inside.

Twenty-Three

"Are you sure she's okay?" Joe asked his brother, who returned alone four hours later, opening the door to Ryan's room and gesturing for Joe to come out into the hall.

"Yeah, she's sleeping. I didn't want to wake her. She took a pretty bad fall from her horse when I found her. I must have spooked them, but she was barely sitting in that saddle. She went in to take a shower while I looked after the horses. When I was finished, I knocked and she didn't answer. I was worried, so I opened the door and walked in, called out to her. I found her lying on her bed. She had never made it to the shower, and she was fast asleep." Logan looked into the room at Ryan. "How's he doing?"

"Ryan's good, just annoyed he can't have pizza. They've got him on broth, which, for a teenager, is about as appealing as a root canal." Joe had napped off and on in the chair beside Ryan's bed, and Ryan had asked repeatedly about Margaret and when she was coming. Joe hadn't told him yet, as she was still with the horses.

"Would you mind staying with Ryan?" Joe asked. "I'd like to get cleaned up."

What he really wanted and needed was to stop in and make sure Margaret was okay. He'd been going out of his mind with worry. The fact was that leaving Margaret alone like he had…well, he felt like a world-class jerk.

"Yeah, you bet. I'll stay," Logan said, tossing a set of keys to Joe. "Take my Jeep, but don't wreck it."

Joe set his hand on Logan's shoulder. "Thank you. Don't let my kid talk you into anything he shouldn't be doing," he said.

Logan's expression changed, and he said, "That Margaret Gordon was torn up about Ryan. She really cares about him. Evidently, she cares about you, too." He pushed open Ryan's door, and Joe stood behind him and watched the excitement light up his son's face when he saw his uncle for the first time in two years.

Joe didn't waste any time leaving. He ended up buying a coffee to go from one of the express carts at the front door, and he was glad for the caffeine buzz, which kept him awake on the drive home. He was just coming up to the driveway that led to the old Spick place and was almost past it when he swung the wheel hard, spinning gravel and sending the back wheels in a tail spin. The Jeep bumped over the ruts, and he spotted all three horses in the corral together. Joe's truck and the horse trailer were right where he had left them. There was no sign of Margaret.

Joe was out of the Jeep when he caught a whiff of something off. He wasn't sure what it was until he lifted his arm and smelled how bad he reeked. Maybe stopping first wasn't such a great idea. He should have gone home, showered, put some clean clothes on, but his need to make sure Margaret was okay overpowered his need to get clean, so he knocked on her door. When he heard nothing, he knocked again and called out, "Margaret!" If she was sleeping, she wouldn't be much longer. He heard a rustling from inside, and she stumbled to the door. When it opened, the first thing he saw was the smudges on her face and the dried blood on her head.

"What the hell happened? Logan said you took a fall, but he didn't tell me you were hurt!" He pushed his way into the house, and Margaret limped, and he watched the way she winced.

"I'm not, really. I fell from the horse, is all," she said. Her hand was shaking as it touched her dark hair, which was in wild disarray.

"Not really? Define 'not really.' I could kick my ass for leaving you out there alone. I was worried sick about you," he said, sliding his hands over both her cheeks. A frown formed between her brows.

"How's Ryan?" she asked, her eyes widening in panic.

"He's fine, complaining because they won't let him have pizza."

She giggled and choked on a sob, and her face scrunched up.

"Hey, what's this?" he said. He wouldn't let her go when she tried to cover her face and a tear leaked out.

"I worried I had hurt him. You don't know what went through my mind. Did I make it worse? Would he wake up? What about his head? He had a bad gash, and he was unconscious. My God, there could have been a brain bleed, swelling, something they missed…." She was shaking.

He held her face between his hands and then slid them over her ears, bringing his face closer. "They took care of everything. You saved his life. He's one lucky kid. They said he only has a concussion, but he has tons of stitches and a busted rib that'll keep him down for a while," he said. He used his thumb to wipe away the dampness under her eyes, wondering what was wrong with him that he had missed how much she loved his son. She hadn't hesitated to walk into danger for him, for his kid, and she had done more than most men could.

"You like to pretend you're so strong, so independent, and you keep everyone away at arm's length, but you're not that tough," he said. "I see through this mask and the role you play for everyone."

She shut her eyes and wouldn't look at him, and she scraped her hand over his. "Joe, don't. You're with someone else, and my heart can't take that. I bleed, I love, and I get hurt over and over, and I can't be. You can't be this nice to me, because you make me think there's more between us, and I…"

He didn't let her finish as he pressed his lips to hers, touching his tongue to her lips. He felt her hesitate, hearing her breath as she allowed him, after a second, to kiss her. When he pulled away, she opened her eyes, showing him her confusion and worry along with a sheen of tears.

"I'm not getting married to Sara, because you were right," he said. "I didn't love her."

She was frowning again. "Why would you want to marry a woman you don't love?"

"Because it was safer. I didn't want to love a woman so much again that if she died, she'd take a part of me with her like Evie did. This time, I knew I wouldn't survive."

She was breathing heavily, thinking, and he could see her mind tossing over a dozen different conclusions. He doubted any of them were right.

"I love you, but I didn't know it until I had you under me and I tasted you, and then you were on me," he said. "I realized it when I was there in the hospital, that I had left you behind. I had chosen between my son and you when I didn't want to make a choice at all. I left you, and I'm sorry."

She reached up and touched his cheek, her hand sliding into his hair. "It wasn't a choice, Joe. You had to go. I wouldn't have let you stay. I had to take the horses back. It wasn't your fault."

He stepped back and dropped his hands, watching her as she leaned against the wall, still in the same clothes they'd started out in two days ago. Her hair was a mess, her face covered in smudges, dirt, and mud. He scooped her up in his arms, and she winced.

"Did I hurt you?" he asked. He held her tight, and she rested her head on his shoulder.

"No, I'm just sore. I meant to have a hot shower, but I laid my head down for a second and fell asleep."

Joe started walking down the hall. He flicked on the light in the bathroom and set her down beside the tub.

"What are you doing?" she asked as he turned on the water and then kicked off his boots.

"Getting you in the shower," he answered.

J oe didn't just get her in the shower after taking off all her clothes—he stripped off his own and joined her under the hot spray. He turned her around and ran his hands over her back. "You're going to have some nice bruises here and here," he said, touching her hip and shoulder. He turned her with all the gentleness she didn't expect and slid his hand into her hair, tilting her head back under the water.

It felt so good, the warmth of the water running in her hair and the warmth of his skin against her chest. She shut her eyes and then opened them when his hands slipped away as he reached for the shampoo and poured some into his hand, running it over her hair and scrubbing the itch. It felt so good.

"You don't need to wash my hair," she said, but she didn't mean it and hoped he wouldn't take his hands off her ever.

"Yeah, I can see how you really mean that," he replied, laughing his low, sexy laugh as he leaned her head back to rinse out the shampoo.

He ran the bar of soap over every inch of her, kneeling down to do her feet, asking her to lift each foot as she leaned on his wide shoulders. When he stood up, he ran his hand over her skin, up her thighs, touching her in the most intimate of places and then setting his hands on her waist. He pulled her to him, and she could feel every inch of his desire for her. He turned, trading places with her under the spray, holding her close as he dunked his head under the nozzle, too low for a man of his height.

He touched his lips to hers and said, "My turn. I'll be quick." He scrubbed his head with shampoo, rinsing it while she grabbed the soap and started running it over his chest, loving the feel of the dark hair that covered it.

The man was amazing with clothes on. With them off, he was godlike.

He set his hand over hers, taking the soap bar. "I'll finish so we can get out of here before it gets cold."

He washed himself quickly, rinsing and turning off the water. He lifted Margaret out of the tub, setting her down and drying her with a towel, taking a closer look at her body as he dried her breasts, her stomach, her legs, taking his time. Only once did she try to cover her breasts with her hands, but he said, "No," moving her hand away and setting his mouth to her nipple.

Margaret gasped and thought her knees would give way as he pressed her against the wall. He pulled away long enough to run the towel over his thick, dark hair and over his body, dumping it on the ground before lifting her in his arms and carrying her to bed, which was a rumpled mess. He set her down with her wet hair on the pillow and moved on top of her.

She instantly moved her legs apart, and he moved his hand between them, touching her and watching her. She took in his expression, which was on fire for her. She ran her hands over his wide, broad shoulders, his perfectly sculpted chest. There was no beer gut on this man, and he had a set of abs. She wondered what he did to keep himself in such good shape. He guided her legs around his waist and leaned over her.

She felt him, so close, entering her slowly. He held himself still, and she said, "Joe, I'm not on birth control." She gasped.

He clenched his teeth and then smiled as he moved and said, "Yeah, I figured as much." He moved again. "I don't plan on letting it matter."

"Joe," she said, right before he set his mouth on hers and deepened the kiss. He moved faster, and she couldn't hold back as he moved again, becoming a part of her and touching her in a way no other man ever had. She screamed out his name as she felt herself lose control and tumble completely over the edge.

Joe woke with the light streaming in the bedroom window and a woman draped half over him. Margaret was sound asleep, and he smiled at how many times they each had awoken during the night. He'd made love to her three times. The last time, he had set her on top of him and let her ride as he played with her breasts, which he'd pictured a hundred times in his head. He had never imagined they would be this perfect.

He ran his hand over her head, and she groaned, running her own hand over his chest and lower. "Hey, good morning," he said.

She blinked and looked up him with a lazy contentedness he'd never seen in her eyes before. She rested her chin on his chest and took a deep breath. "We should go see Ryan," she said.

He ran his hand over her dark, tangled hair, just watching her. When she sucked in her lower lip nervously, he could tell she was starting to pull away.

"We will," he said, running his hand over her back and down lower. "Are you sore?"

He smiled when she blushed, and he rolled her over, the sheets tangling around them. His cell phone buzzed, and he dropped his head and groaned, "Great timing."

"Go answer it, Joe," Margaret urged him. "It could be important."

Joe slipped out of bed and went into the bathroom, where his clothes were still in a heap on the floor. He pulled the cell phone from his pocket. "Yeah?" he said.

"It's Logan. Just checking to see if you got lost."

Joe didn't miss the hint of mischief in his brother's voice. "How's Ryan?" he asked. He could hear the bed squeak and then Margaret's footsteps on the floor.

"He's wondering what happened to his dad. He's kind of worried. I think he believes you may have taken off and married that blonde who left her handprint on your face."

Joe heard the floor squeak behind him and watched as Margaret tied a blue housecoat closed. "Tell him I'm with Margaret and we'll be up soon."

"Oh," his brother said with a chuckle. "Sorry to wake you."

Joe hung up and noticed the blush rise on Margaret's face as he stood naked in her house in front of her. He stepped closer to her. "Ready to go see Ryan?"

She smiled with such shyness that he wanted to laugh at her. "Just need to feed the horses first, and you need to get some clean clothes," she said, setting her hand playfully on his chest.

He set his over hers, pulling her closer. "I do, so I guess we'd best hurry," he agreed. He wrapped his arms around her waist and lifted her, giving her a proper good-morning kiss.

Twenty-Six

J oe walked hand in hand with Margaret into the hospital. He didn't miss the way she had tensed the closer they got or the way she seemed to be sweating as they stepped through the doors. He was positive that at one time, she would have been as comfortable here as he was on his spread, milling lumber. "You okay?" he asked, looking down at her and squeezing her hand as she leaned closer to him.

"Yeah. You know, it's silly," she said. She darted a quick glance at him and then away, and although she tried, she couldn't hide her discomfort from him.

"It's not silly. It was a pretty big deal, Margaret, and it gutted you, so give yourself a break."

He saw the lump in her throat move as she swallowed and blinked rapidly. He pulled her into his arms when he reached the elevator bank and punched the button, kissing the top of her head and just holding her while she trembled and then took a deep breath, seeming to pull herself together.

When the elevator doors opened, he put his arm

around her and walked her in. She looked so cute with her dark hair in a ponytail. He could see the freckles on her nose, and he loved that she didn't have a stitch of makeup on. With her complexion, she didn't need it.

The elevator dinged on the second floor, and the door opened. Two doctors stepped in, and Joe could feel Margaret stiffen, so he tightened his arm around her, squeezing her shoulder. She glanced his way but didn't look at him. A short ride later, on the third floor, he nudged her out of the elevator.

She took a deep breath. "So which room is Ryan in?" she asked.

"The first room, right here." He went to push open the door, his arm still around Margaret, when she slid around and set her hand on his chest, looking up at him.

"Joe, what are we going to tell Ryan?" she said.

For a minute, she looked a little panicked, and he wanted to laugh until he felt her hand shaking again on his chest. "It'll be fine. Relax," he said. "What are you worried about?"

"Well, last Ryan knew, you were marrying Sara. Did you tell him it was off? Although he likes me, how do you think he's going to react?" She was looking at him with wide eyes and a helpless expression.

"I think you're not giving my kid enough credit. I think this is exactly what he needs to hear. We're together now. He'll be happy."

"Well, maybe we should talk first about exactly what this 'together' looks like," she said.

What the hell was she doing? They had already settled this, so why was she stirring things up? For a minute, he was positive she was so bent on self-destruction that she was deliberately trying to start a fight with him. "What are you doing? We've already settled this. I love you, and you love me. End of story, or is there something more? Have you decided that a struggling millworker who takes jobs here and there to make ends meet isn't enough for you? I'm not a rich man. My bank balance the end of each month is close to zero. I've learned to fix things myself because I don't have money to throw around. Maybe we should have talked about that."

She moved back, pulling her hand away as if he had slapped her. She firmed her lips and set her jaw, and there was a spark in her eyes that let him know she was now good and mad. "I'm not some moneygrubber. I don't care if you have nothing. Money is nice, but it's not what drives me or what I'm looking for, and it can't make you happy."

"That's interesting you would say that, considering I watched you and your mother fighting over just that thing, good ol' money, the day you buried your grandfather." Of course the moment he said it he wanted to take it back.

"What?" she said. Before she could add anything else, Ryan's door opened and Logan gave him a look as if he'd heard everything.

"Ryan's been waiting for you two. Hey, Margaret, how're you feeling?" he said.

She seemed to need a minute to pull herself together. She shook her head, glanced down the hallway, and then into the room at Ryan. She gave Joe her back and said to Logan, "I'm fine, just a little sore, but I'll be good as new in a few days. I never got a chance to thank you for coming to help me. I don't know what I would have done if you hadn't shown up when you did. Thanks for looking after the horses, too."

Logan gave her one of his flirty smiles and winked at her, and Joe wanted to pop him one. "You're welcome, but I'm pretty sure you would have made it. You're a capable woman. Haven't seen too many with the grit and determination you have. I admire that. I was just glad I could help a lovely lady like you."

Joe felt her instantly soften to Logan, and he wanted to reach over and shake his brother. Didn't he realize Margaret was his?

"Hey, Ryan. How are you feeling, honey?" Margaret said, ducking under Logan's arm and going to Ryan's side.

When Joe tried to step into the room, Logan blocked his way. "We could hear you two arguing. What gives?" he said.

Joe was still mad at his big brother, still irritated with Margaret and his own inability to check his mouth. What could ever have possessed him to say what he did? "She's not available," he said, jabbing his finger into his brother's chest.

Logan allowed a teasing smile to touch his lips. "Oh, man, are you in trouble," he said. He stepped back, but before Joe could step past him, he said, "Word of advice, there, little brother. If you want this woman, you need to respect her. What I heard of that little bit," he shook his head, "that was really stupid."

Joe growled and stepped around his brother. Ryan's gaze immediately went from Margaret to him. His face was still pale, with some bruising on his forehead and cheek. Margaret was reading the chart and ignoring Joe. "How are you feeling this morning?" he asked.

"Sore—and hungry. Dad, when are they going to let me have some real food?"

Margaret seemed to be satisfied with what she had read and closed up the chart. She set it back at the foot of the bed. "I'll talk to them. I don't see why you can't have some-thing today. What do you want?"

"I want a burger, fries, a milkshake…" he started as his eyes got big and hopeful.

"Yeah, that's not going to happen, Ryan," Margaret said. "You had a major trauma. They'll probably let you have something solid and move off Jell-O today." She didn't look at Joe, and he noticed how she moved to the other side of the bed, away from him.

"Ryan, I wanted to apologize," Joe started, and Margaret's gaze became worried as she watched him, obviously nervous about what he was going to say. "Sara and I aren't getting married. I shouldn't have asked her, and I did it only because I thought you needed a mother. That wasn't fair of me."

"I don't need a mother. Are you still dating her?" Ryan added.

"No. We're done. You won't be seeing her again."

He breathed a sigh of relief, and then he looked worried again. "But you're still dating. Are you going to look for someone else online?"

"No, my online days are over," Joe said, watching as Margaret rolled her eyes. Well, what did she expect him to say?

"Well, that's good," Ryan said.

"What if I met someone you really like?" Joe began. He watched the way Ryan looked away as if disappointed, expecting the worst. What if he'd been wrong? He knew Ryan liked Margaret a lot, but maybe he wasn't ready for his father to date at all. For a minute, Joe relived the choice he had made, leaving Margaret alone with the horses as he hopped into the chopper with his son. It was a choice he never thought he'd have to make again.

"You know what, Ryan?" Margaret rested her hand on his arm before Joe could say another word. "I don't think you're going to have to worry about your dad bringing someone home any time soon."

Ryan looked to her with relief, and then he said, "Is Storm okay?"

Margaret gave Joe a warning glance, and Joe rocked back on his heels. He couldn't believe Ryan wasn't jumping up and down, excited that he and Margaret were together. It sickened him when he realized his son held the power to come between him and Margaret.

"Storm is fine. He's not hurt. But, Ryan, that was a very foolish thing to do. You could have been killed, and this isn't just about the fact that you took off on Storm, who you had no business riding. You took off in the dead of night, in circumstances that had you running on pure emotion. Didn't we go over this? How did you get him saddled, anyway, without me hearing?"

Ryan flushed, and it was the first bit of color Joe had seen in his face since the accident. "I'm sorry. I wasn't thinking. I was mad, and I was tired of listening to Dad and Sara in his room. It hurt that he had picked her over me."

Joe felt himself reeling, and he had the good grace to blush. He felt Logan watching him, and when he glanced over and shrugged, his brother shook his head as if he should have known better.

"I didn't think, I just snuck in. I was scared, but I saddled him, remembering how you were with him. You didn't let your fear show, and I tried to do what you did. I only thought about leaving. I didn't think of where I was going, just rode and rode for hours, and I fell off when Storm spooked. All I could think about was that I didn't think Dad loved me." He sounded so hurt that Joe wondered what he had done to make his son believe that.

"Ryan, are you kidding me?" Joe barked. "I would choose you over any woman. I'll stay alone forever if that's what you want. You're more important to me. How could you even think that?"

Margaret stepped back and shoved her hands in her pockets. She wouldn't look at him.

Ryan turned his head toward his dad, his pillow rustling. He frowned as if trying to figure out what his dad was saying. "You really mean it?" he said.

Joe looked at Margaret again and had a sinking feeling she believed he'd just tossed her to the curb. In fact, that was exactly what he had just done, and he couldn't seem to get out from under how badly he was messing this up.

"Ryan, listen, what I really want you to know…"

"Dad, you didn't mean it, did you?" Ryan said. His son really didn't believe in him.

Joe leaned over, pressing his hand on the pillow beside him. "You listen to me. I meant it. If I date again, you'll get a say. You want me alone, you just say so."

Ryan firmed his lips and said, "Dad, do you think for a while you could stay off all those dating sites, take your profile down, and not date anyone?"

Joe watched the uncertainty in his son's eyes and knew this would be a make-or-break moment with him. He loved him, and all the happiness he had felt moments ago with Margaret seemed to slip through his fingers as if everything had suddenly turned to dust.

When he looked up, Margaret had stepped away and was looking out the window of the hospital room as if lost in thought. He also knew he couldn't take one step toward her or touch her right now. His brother stood at the foot of the bed, looking from Margaret to him and back to Ryan, and he opened his mouth as if to say something but didn't.

"Ryan, I just wanted to come by and see how you are," Margaret said. "I want you to get some rest. I'll leave you and your dad here to spend time together. Remember what

I said about Storm. You need to really think about whether you're up to the challenge with him. He's not an easy horse, and he'll never be easy."

"But you'll help me, right? You're still going to work with Storm, aren't you?" Ryan asked, sounding so hopeful.

"Ryan, when you get out of here and you're feeling better, we'll talk more about that," she said. She patted his arm, and with the way she looked down on him in those few seconds, Joe wondered how he'd missed her feelings for his son. The woman showed every emotion on her face, in her eyes, and she really cared for Ryan. "I'm going to go," she said.

"Are you going to come back?" Ryan asked.

Joe watched her response and could see the walls she had continually stuck up around herself. They were stronger than ever, but this was the first time they were up for Ryan. He wondered if his son picked up on it, too.

"I have things to do, Ryan, a lot of messes to clean up after looking for you. You just rest. I'll see you soon," she said. She stepped around Logan, and he darted a glance at her. Joe started after her, but she just shook her head. "No, Joe, stay. I can find my own way home."

"I'll take you home," Logan piped up, holding out his hand to Joe. "Keys," he said, and the look he gave him said loud and clear that he was an idiot and his brother had a few choice words for him. Joe watched as his brother followed the one woman he could never have out the door.

I t had been three weeks since Ryan's accident. For the past week, Ryan had bounced back until he was almost his old self. Today was the first day he returned to school. Logan had stayed on and spent time with Ryan, helping Joe mill wood. He had even gone to get the horses from Margaret without one word. Joe was grateful that Logan hadn't brought up Margaret even after driving her home.

Joe had only asked once about Margaret when Logan came back to the hospital that morning. Logan had given him a hard look and said, "She's a strong woman. She's home safe. Leave her alone. You made your choice, and I think you've done enough."

And he had, so he left her alone, but every night and every moment during the day, Margaret invaded his thoughts, leaving him short tempered and miserable.

Joe was driving home after taking Ryan to school and spending half an hour talking with his teachers, as well as the kids who were interested in the coolness of the helicopter rescue and Ryan's near-death experience. Of course, Ryan milked the drama for all it was worth.

Every time Joe drove past the entrance to Margaret's spread, he suffered from an unbearable ache. He couldn't put into words that hollowed-out feeling that left him weak, a feeling of loss so deep it took everything he had to get up in the morning, the same feeling he'd had after losing Evie.

A red and white sign beckoned at the side of her driveway: "For sale." Joe stomped on the brake, the back end of the truck skidding sideways, and he just about hit the ditch. Of every imaginable scenario that had gone through his mind, this wasn't one of them.

He rested his hand over his mouth, his truck still idling. He shut his eyes for a second, trying to decide what to do. It was probably best to just go home. To hell with her. This hurt worse than anything, even though he realized she was probably running again. Wasn't that what she did so well?

He started down her driveway. The entire time, that little voice in his head said, *This is a bad idea.* He kept going, his palms sweating as he wondered what he would say when he saw her. I'm sorry? Geez, that somehow felt so meaningless. All those thoughts seemed to vanish when he saw his brother's Jeep. Margaret placed her hand over her eyes to cut the glare from the sun and see who was coming, and Logan never took his eyes from Joe as he brought his truck within inches of his brother before stopping. Anyone else would have dived out of the way. Even Margaret was looking a little freaked out by how close he had come to hitting his brother. Joe was out of his vehicle, and Logan did nothing but raise his eyebrows and say, "Are you lost?"

He was a man on the edge, and, for the first time, he felt his brother taunting him. Was he really making moves on Margaret, seriously? He walked up to his brother and shoved him, and Logan lost his balance and stumbled back.

"Hey, what's the matter with you, Joe?" Margaret shouted as she tried to put herself between the brothers.

Logan put his hands on her shoulders and said, "Margaret, don't get in the middle of this."

"The hell I won't. This is my place. If you two want to behave like two imbeciles, then take it somewhere else. Joe, why are you here?" she snapped, stepping away when he went to touch her.

Logan moved his hand in front of Margaret and then took a step, and Joe didn't miss the purely protective move from a would-be suitor. He wanted to deck him. What the hell was he doing, moving in on Margaret?

"Hey!" Margaret shouted from behind him. "Logan, I can take care of myself. Joe, why are you here?"

He fisted his hands and pumped them once, twice. He watched Logan, wondering when his brother had become such a prick. He finally glanced at Margaret, who was watching him with a range of emotions but only one he recognized: hurt.

"I saw your for-sale sign. What are you doing, Margaret? Your grandfather, your family is buried here, right over there." He jabbed his arm out, because it was the only excuse he could think of for her not to sell.

She didn't flinch when she said, "You have to learn when you're done, and I think it's time to move on. I need a fresh start. I can't hide out here. I have no reason to stay anymore." She appeared so sad, and she worked her jaw before asking, "How's Ryan?"

"He's been asking why you haven't come to see him, and he's anxious about Storm. He wants to start working with him again. He thinks you're going to help him." Joe added that last bit more for him, because he wanted Margaret in his life. The fact was that Ryan had asked Joe if he'd drive him to Margaret's, and Joe had made a pile of excuses every day because he couldn't face Margaret after what he'd done. Ryan didn't know what had happened between him and Margaret and how close they really were. Joe couldn't hide his feelings, and he was pretty sure Ryan would have picked up on the unease between them.

"Yes, Logan told me, and I'm going to tell you the same thing I told Logan: I can't help with Storm. You're going to have to find someone else. I've done all I can for him, and considering…" She coughed, but he could tell it was a pathetic cover for her emotions. He realized what she had said about Logan, and it confused him. Why would Logan try to get her to work with Storm?

"Look, Margaret, can I talk to you alone?" he said.

She started shaking her head, and her face was so tight he could tell she was holding herself together. Logan wasn't moving. In fact, he crossed his arms and looked toward her. "Margaret, just say the word and I'll have him leave," he said.

"What is your problem, Logan? Seriously, she's not your woman," Joe barked.

"And she's not yours, either. You made sure of that, so maybe you should just move on." Logan took a step toward Joe, and Margaret slapped a hand on both their chests.

"Joe, I'll give you five minutes," she snapped. "Logan, please excuse us."

Just feeling the warmth of her hand on his chest had him wanting to pull her against him.

Logan jabbed a finger his way in warning and stepped back, limping a couple steps toward the barn before pausing to give Joe another warning look and stepping inside.

Margaret looked anywhere but at him. She was finally forced to look his way as the silence became unbearable between them. He went to slide his hand on her shoulder, but she sidestepped, deliberately moving out of reach. "Don't, please," she said.

"Look, I realize saying I'm sorry doesn't make up for what I did. I just didn't feel I had a choice. Maybe with time…"

"Stop right there, Joe. Ryan has to be your first priority. You screwed up once already. You can't do it again, and I knew someone was going to get hurt. I just never imagined it would turn out like this."

"Please don't sell and leave," Joe pleaded.

She looked him square in the eye. "I have to. I can't stay here. You're too much of a reminder of what I can't have, and it's not just Ryan. You don't really trust me. After all, what did you say about fighting with my mother over money when my grandfather wasn't even in the ground yet?"

He looked away and blinked, fighting to hold back his emotions. He still couldn't believe he'd said that. "I'm sorry, Margaret. When I heard you that day, fighting with your mother…"

"Well, you didn't stick around long enough to hear everything. If you really knew me, you'd know it was never about the money. Mom wanted to sell this, and she was going to contest the will. She figured it should all go to her, being the only daughter, but Granddad knew this place meant nothing to Mom—it never did. That was why he left it to me, because Mom wouldn't have just sold it, she'd have subdivided all this land and sold it off piece by piece, whatever it took to destroy it. Deep down, she hated her father. I just never knew how much until the day of his funeral, when she told me her plans. I guess she never expected me to stand up to her like I did, but then, she doesn't really know me. For her, it was about the money, but for me it was about keeping this land intact." She let out a slow breath and looked around, squinting.

"If that's the truth, why are you selling now?" he asked.

"Because of you," she said. "I'll only let it go on the condition the buyer won't subdivide."

"You can't guarantee that," he argued.

"Well, actually, yes, I can. I've already filed a covenant on this land."

He didn't want this to be it. He watched this woman whom he had misjudged so badly. He didn't think he could take losing her. "Is there any chance you could be pregnant?" he said. He prayed, wanting it and worrying about it at the same time.

She stared at him for the longest time and said, "Good news, Joe: I'm not." She looked away and then cleared her throat. "Goodbye," she said, starting to walk away.

This time, he let her.

———

Margaret went around the side of the house and pressed her back against the rough wood, listening to Joe's truck pull away. She couldn't hold back the tears. She'd cried into her pillow every night since walking out of Ryan's hospital room. She couldn't believe how easily Joe had let her go, though she knew why he had done it, and she understood. She tried telling that to her heart, which couldn't understand why this man wasn't kicking down the door and coming for her. She wanted a different outcome. She wanted Joe, and to be a mother to Ryan, but maybe too much had happened, and Ryan needed his dad all to himself for a while.

The fact was that Margaret didn't have a clue whether she was pregnant or not. It was too early, but she prayed every night for at least that one small gift. If she was, she'd start over someplace new, just her and her child, because she didn't know whether she'd ever be able to take another chance on love. She was unlucky, for sure. When she finally realized she had found the one she'd been looking for her whole life, instead of everything working out, their love story had been reminiscent of all the great love stories throughout history, ending in heartache and tragedy.

A hand touched her shoulder, and she jumped and set her arm over her eyes, not wanting Logan to see her like this. The man didn't give her a chance to push him away, as he slid his arm around her and pulled her into a great big hug. He held her shoulders while she sobbed.

"Margaret, I love my brother, but sometimes he can be a misguided fool," Logan said as he rubbed her back. "Shh, it'll be all right."

She nodded, but as she gripped Logan's shirt and struggled through her tears, she wondered how it would ever be all right again.

J oe hadn't said one word on the drive home with Ryan, and when they drove past Margaret's and he saw the for-sale sign, he leaned forward and asked in a panicky voice, "Dad, is Margaret selling?"

"Yeah" was all he could manage to say as he narrowed his eyes and kept driving past.

When he pulled in at home, Logan was walking out of the house with his duffle bag over his shoulder, tossing it in the back of his Jeep.

"Uncle Logan, are you leaving?" Ryan shouted. He started toward his uncle, moving a lot faster than he had all week.

Logan set his hand on Ryan's shoulder and glanced over and up at Joe. "Yeah, I thought I better, before I wear out my welcome here. Besides, you and your dad got some things you need to sort out and work through. You don't need me hanging around." Logan glanced over at Joe again.

"Uncle Logan, why is everyone leaving? Even Margaret has a for-sale sign up."

Logan didn't take his eyes off Joe when he answered. "Sometimes, a person has to learn when it's time to move on. I've got my own life to get back to, and Margaret… well, she feels it's something she has to do."

"But I don't want Margaret to go!" Ryan said. "I guess I kind of hoped Dad would like her as much as I do. I thought he'd take a liking to her, and maybe one day he'd marry her. She's my friend. She listens to me."

Joe was still stuck on the part where Ryan had said he should marry Margaret. His ears were ringing, and he wondered for a moment what kind of stupid look was on his face when his brother started laughing at him.

Logan turned Ryan around to face him. "Ryan, you need to tell your dad exactly what you just told me."

The look on Ryan's face was priceless. "Dad, what's wrong with you? You've got a weird look on your face."

"Ryan, are you telling me that if I told you Margaret and I were dating and I'd like to marry her, you'd be happy?"

Ryan looked back at his uncle as if he couldn't understand what his dad was asking. "Well, yeah. I mean, if you'd really like to marry Margaret, I think it would be kind of cool." Ryan jammed his hands in his pockets and shrugged in his awkward teenage way.

"Ryan, in the hospital you said you didn't want me dating anyone," Joe said accusingly.

Ryan frowned. "No, I said I didn't want you dating Sara or doing that online dating anymore," he said, as if his meaning had been obvious. Then he got a hopeful look on his face. "Dad, are you going to marry Margaret?"

Logan rolled his eyes and shook his head. For the first time, Joe wondered how in the hell he was going to fix this. "That's the plan, if I didn't screw this up too bad," he replied. He looked to Logan. "Any ideas?"

"Yeah, try apologizing," Logan quipped. "Then, when that doesn't work, beg."

Joe jumped in his truck and started it, rolling down his window and leaning out. "Hey, Logan, can you stay a bit?"

Logan just waved his hand and said, "Go, get your girl." He set his hand on Ryan's shoulder, and Joe hoped that when he got to Margaret, it wouldn't be too late.

Twenty~Nine

Margaret was just going into the house after tossing a flake of hay to Angel when she heard the truck coming up her driveway, and not just any truck—Joe's truck.

After the roller coaster he'd put her through, she didn't think she could be nice anymore. Joe had always been really good at schmoozing, telling stories, and working things in his favor. Whatever he wanted now, she was done hearing it. The fact was that all she had ever wanted was that fairytale ending, to have it all. Wasn't that what every girl wanted? But Joe had proven time and again that he was no good, and definitely no good for her.

When he got out of his truck, he dug into each step as he walked right toward her. Margaret skidded down the stairs and started to move sideways. The look in his eyes as he stalked her was like that of a predatory cat. Her heart was pounding the closer he got, and she looked right and then left, with nowhere to run. Then he was on her just as she took that first step to bolt, tossing her over his shoulders and setting his hand on her rump. He was walking her back to his truck when her good sense finally kicked in.

"Joe, put me down, now!" she shouted. She grabbed his waist as he jostled her and slid her down so she felt every inch of him.

He set both his hands on her cheeks and leaned in to kiss her, and she started to kiss him back but then set her hands on his chest and pushed. No matter how badly she wanted him, she couldn't have him. "Don't," she snapped.

He stepped back, letting her go. Her breathing was fast and heavy as she watched this man who confused the hell out of her and had broken her heart, a man who could reduce her to nothing.

"We're getting married as soon as possible," he said.

"What?" she blurted out, unable to believe what he was saying. Had he lost his mind?

"Ryan was devastated that you would consider leaving, and he told me he didn't mean you—I mean, me not dating you." Joe was actually smiling, and it was the first time she had ever considered hurting someone.

"Seriously, Joe?" She shook her head. "You know it was just a matter of time before I discovered you're no good for me. Your lips talk sweet and then turn into vinegar at the snap of a finger, and then you toss me to the curb. I feel like a yoyo. I always knew you were selfish, but this isn't all about you and when you want something." She waved her finger at him. "Well, let me tell you something: You're no longer getting the chance to break my heart! I've ripped off the blinders and really see you."

She stepped away again. "I love you, Joe, but you're letting Ryan run your life—a kid! You screwed up, but now he says, 'Jump, marry this woman,' and you run after me and say, 'Oh, hey, Margaret, it's okay now. We're getting married'?" She ran her hand over her head. "No." Her hand was shaking, so she fisted it in her hair. "No, this girl has pulled on her big-girl pants and her goodbye shoes, and she's walking away." She started back to the house, giving him her back, when he touched her arm.

"Margaret, please forgive me for treating you so badly. You deserve everything good, and you deserve to be loved so deeply. You don't deserve how I treated you. I swear, Margaret, if you'll give me a chance, you won't regret it. I promise you, I'll always stand by you, by your side. I'll love you as you deserve to be loved, and I swear I won't take you for granted. What I didn't realize before and I know now is that you're the one I've looked for, the one who can heal my heart, the only one I want to spend the rest of my life with. Please, Margaret, if you'll have me…"

She turned until she faced Joe, slowly looking up. Her breath caught when she glimpsed a sheen of tears in his eyes.

"Margaret, I screwed up with Ryan, all because I wanted love. I just didn't know how to find it. Then you, in that ridiculous hat, with your attitude…well, you had me. I was terrified, but I don't want to be scared anymore. Ryan isn't running our lives, and I promise to try not to screw up again, though I guarantee you I will. Through all of it, I'll never stop loving you."

"I need a guarantee, Joe," she said.

"You can't have one. You just have to have faith that it'll all work out. You have to stop running."

She took a breath when he held out his hand to her, and her heart softened. She pressed her hands over her mouth when she realized he truly meant every word he'd said. Finally, she slid her trembling hand in his.

Margaret could hear the violin strings and the first stirring notes of the wedding song she'd chosen, "I'll Stand by You." The guitar joined in, and she started out of the back room of the church. Stan Jerow was waiting for her in his green suit and string tie, grinning ear to ear like her father, who should have been here. She'd emailed him and her mother but had only received a brisk, congratulatory email from Italy saying he was unable to attend her wedding on such short notice, considering it was only three days from when Joe had shown up at her grandfather's house.

"You look so beautiful," Stan said. She had to lean her cheek down to let him kiss her, since he was two inches shorter. Margaret was wearing a simple white sheath that ended just at her knees, the only thing she could find in Post Falls.

"Could my mother make it?" she asked, but Stan just shook his head.

"I'm sorry, honey. Hazel's kept an eye out for her."

"It's all right. She never answered my email. For all I

know, she's vacationing somewhere or busy with some business deal." She tried to make light of the hurt, but Stan wasn't buying any of it.

"Your granddad would be proud of you today, and I like to think he's looking down on you and smiling," he said, beaming up at her.

She held the bouquet of wildflowers Hazel had brought. When the doors to the church opened and Margaret looked down the aisle, there was Joe in a dark suit, his hair slicked back, with Ryan beside him. She gasped when she took in all four of his brothers, tall, hunky, and standing shoulder to shoulder. "Oh, my Lord, those brothers of his are going to have all the women fighting each other to get to them," she said.

Stan just patted her hand. "They have been for years, honey, but one of them is now off the market for good."

"You got that right," she said with a laugh.

"You ready?" Stan asked.

"More than ready," she replied, and she started down the aisle to become Mrs. Joe Wilde.

Turn the page for a sneak peek of
FRIENDLY FIRE the next book in THE WILDE BROTHERS
Available in AUDIOBOOK, PAPERBACK & eBOOK

**When Logan Wilde takes a job as a sheriff in a
small Idaho town, he expects a quiet, peaceful life
that will bore him to tears...until he walks
through the door of Julia Cooper's cafe.**

In FRIENDLY FIRE, after a roadside bomb ends his
career in the marines, Logan Wilde struggles to put his life
back together, taking a job as a sheriff in a small Idaho
town. He expects a quiet, peaceful life that will bore him to
tears. Until he walks through the door of Julia Cooper's
cafe.

From the moment the new sheriff walks into Julia's cafe,
she fights the attraction from the new sheriff, a man she
recognizes is ex-military and has baggage that comes along
with it. Even though she's never felt this way for another
man, Julia isn't willing to take a chance with Logan. No
she's convinced herself she needs stability, someone average, someone who has never handled a gun. Except when
her daughter disappears its Logan who's there for her, it's
Logan she turns to, and Logan who turns the town upside
down searching for her.

But what Logan realizes is the disappearance of her
daughter may not be as it seems, and while Julia waits on
the sidelines she wonders if she'll ever be able to trust
again and open her heart and take a chance on love.

Chapter 1

Don't choke, don't hesitate, the voice in his head urged over and over as Logan Wilde pounded the ground, kicking up dust and sand as he ran through the field, his finger locked on his rifle. As the squad leader, he was never supposed to go first, but he wanted—needed—to; even though his heart was pounding. Adrenaline surged through his veins like cool liquid from an IV. Sweat made his T-shirt and uniform stick to his chest, a second skin…and the smell, it was something he might never forget. The dirt and grit scraped his lungs, his nose, his mouth. He had been told he would get used to it eventually.

The heat and dirt and grunge didn't get to him, though, no matter how uncomfortable they were. What got to him was the guilt and worry, needing to be first through the door, because if anyone was going to take a bullet, it had to be him. These were his men. He had trained them, and they were his brothers.

He hunkered down, resting his rifle on the sandy mound and looking through his scope, eyeing the roadblock ahead as his marines took their position. His men all knew what to do. Many of them were still kids, but they trained together and lived together, and they knew each other better than most families. To Logan, these men *were* family. He didn't have to look to know that Sergeant Mike Duffy was manning the tank-mounted machine gun or that Corporal Jeff Starly had his back.

He gave the order right before a high-pitched whistle caught his attention—then there was a flash, heat and pain. His muscles seized at the long, rough droning sound, intense pain ripping through his leg. He gasped, fighting past the sense of being strangled. He couldn't get his breath. His eyes were open, and he was on his back, staring up at the light blue sky. Was it the sky? He blinked. The sound was deafening; everything happening in slow motion. Where was the brightness, the obscured sun, and the colorless desert? It made no sense, this dingy, speckled ceiling.

He blinked again. The buzzing kept going on and on, irritating him. It just wouldn't stop. His heartbeat was a booming sound in his ears, and something twisted around his legs, pulling him down. This time, he couldn't get away. He was drowning, he was sure. Something had him, and he thrashed and fought. There was a crash, then silence. No noise, no buzz—nothing. He just stared. Logan blinked, trying to make sense of what he was seeing.

He took a breath, beads of sweat rolling off his forehead as he tried to swallow past the dryness in his throat—his heart hammering in his chest. When he went to lift his hand, twisted in the sheets, he yanked it free and heard the cloth tear. He was naked, out of breath as if he'd been running for miles, and he was drenched with sweat. His face, his chest, even his hands were damp. He stared at a spot on the wall and then lower, to a shattered black alarm clock in the corner, then to his gun on the nightstand beside him.

Logan Wilde lowered his face to his hands and scrubbed hard over a day-old beard. "Get a grip," he muttered, his hands trembling as he tried to shake off the dream that returned every time he closed his eyes. He never knew when the dream would hit him. It always crept up on him, sucking him back into the insanity of war. It took him a minute now, as he stood on shaky legs, staring at the plain, boxlike bedroom, his clothes stacked on a three-drawer dresser, before it started to come back to him. He had taken a job in MacKay, a small town, part of a ranching community nestled in a charming valley with Idaho's nine highest peaks right at its back door.

This should have given him peace. MacKay had everything he wanted, everything he needed. He had told himself over and over that this would be good for him. He took in the rumpled double bed, nightstand, and dresser that had come with the older two-bedroom house he was renting at the edge of town. It was all he needed, since it was already furnished with everything, including a coffeepot in the kitchen. It was perfect, no stress, easy: So why was he still having these damn dreams?

He sat back on the edge of the bed, the mattress dipping, and lowered his head in his hands. He ran his fingers roughly through his short, rumpled hair and over the back of his head. His damn hands still wouldn't quit shaking. He held them up in front of his face, worried for a minute that he'd see blood; and let out a sigh of relief when he didn't. He blinked, sweat rolling off his brow and down the bridge of his nose. His large, calloused, tanned hands should have been steady and sure and solid—instead he felt like some wet-behind-the-ears kid.

"Get a grip. Come on, it's not real," he said, his gruff

voice sounding strange to his own ears. He was a man on the edge; losing control. He had dangled between life and death, seeing all the horrors of battle. He had teetered with one foot over that edge during the seventeen days he had been in a coma; tubes sticking out of him, a ventilator breathing for him. He had been left without a spleen, his skull fractured, his leg having to be pieced back together—all because of the roadside bomb he had never spotted. The explosion had ended his career as a first sergeant in the marines, but that wasn't the worst of it. No, the worst thing was his memories of the people he had lost because of that mistake.

"Lorhainne Eckhart is one of my go to authors when I want a guaranteed good book. So many twists and turns, but also so much love and such a strong sense of family."

(LORA W., REVIEWER)

New York Times & USA Today bestseller Lorhainne Eckhart is best known for writing Raw Relatable Real Romance where "Morals and family are running themes." As one fan calls her, she is the "Queen of the family saga." (aherman) writing "the ups and downs of what goes on within a family but also with some suspense, angst and of course a bit of romance thrown in for good measure."

Follow Lorhainne on Bookbub to receive alerts on New Releases and Sales and join her mailing list at Lorhainne-Eckhart.com for her Monday Blog, all book news, give-aways and FREE reads. With over 120 books, audiobooks, and multiple series published and available at all, retailers now translated into six languages. She is a multiple recipient of the Readers' Favorite Award for Suspense and Romance, and lives in the Pacific Northwest on an island, is the mother of three, her oldest has autism and she is an advocate for never giving up on your dreams.

"Lorhainne Eckhart has this uncanny way of just hitting the spot every time with her books."

(CAROLINE L., REVIEWER)

The O'Connells: *The O'Connells of Livingston, Montana are not your typical family. A riveting collection of stories surrounding the ups and downs of what goes on within a family but also with some suspense, angst and of course a bit of romance thrown in for good measure. "I thought I loved the Friessens, but I absolutely adore the O'Connell's. Each and every book has different genres of stories, but the one thing in common is how she is able to wrap it around the family, which is the heart of each story." (C. Logue)*

The Friessens: *An emotional big family romance series, the Friessen family siblings find their relationships tested, lay their hearts on the line, and discover lasting love! "Lorhainne Eckhart is one of my go to authors when I want* *a guaranteed good book. So many twists and turns, but also so much love and such a strong sense of family." (Lora W., Reviewer)*

The Parker Sisters: *The Parker Sisters are a close-knit family, and like any other family they have their ups and downs. Eckhart has crafted another intense family drama… "The character development is outstanding, and the emotional investment is high…" (Aherman, Reviewer)*

The McCabe Brothers: *Join the five McCabe siblings on their journeys to the dark and dangerous side of love! An intense, exhilarating collection of romantic thrillers you won't want to miss. — "Eckhart has a new series that is definitely worth the read. The queen of the family saga started this series with a spin-off of her wildly successful Friessen series." From a Readers' Favorite award—winning author and "queen of the family saga" (Aherman)*

Lorhainne loves to hear from her readers! You can connect with me at:
www.LorhainneEckhart.com
lorhainneeckhart.le@gmail.com

Also by Lorhainne Eckhart

The Outsider Series
The Forgotten Child (Brad and Emily)
A Baby and a Wedding *(An Outsider Series Short)*
Fallen Hero (Andy, Jed, and Diana)
The Search *(An Outsider Series Short)*
The Awakening (Andy and Laura)
Secrets (Jed and Diana)
Runaway (Andy and Laura)
Overdue *(An Outsider Series Short)*
The Unexpected Storm (Neil and Candy)
The Wedding (Neil and Candy)

The Friessens: A New Beginning
The Deadline (Andy and Laura)
The Price to Love (Neil and Candy)
A Different Kind of Love (Brad and Emily)
A Vow of Love, A Friessen Family Christmas

The Friessens
The Reunion
The Bloodline (Andy & Laura)
The Promise (Diana & Jed)
The Business Plan (Neil & Candy)
The Decision (Brad & Emily)
First Love (Katy)
Family First
Leave the Light On
In the Moment

In the Family
In the Silence
In the Charm
Unexpected Consequences
It Was Always You
The First Time I Saw You
Welcome to My Arms
Welcome to Boston
I'll Always Love You
Ground Rules
A Reason to Breathe
You Are My Everything
Anything For You
The Homecoming
Stay Away From My Daughter
The Bad Boy
A Place of Our Own
The Visitor
All About Devon
Long Past Dawn
How to Heal a Heart
Keep Me In Your Heart

The O'Connells
The Neighbor
The Third Call
The Secret Husband
The Quiet Day
The Commitment
The Missing Father
The Hometown Hero
Justice
The Family Secret

The Fallen O'Connell
The Return of the O'Connells
And The She Was Gone
The Stalker
The O'Connell Family Christmas
The Girl Next Door
Broken Promises
The Gatekeeper
The Hunted

The McCabe Brothers
Don't Stop Me (Vic)
Don't Catch Me (Chase)
Don't Run From Me (Aaron)
Don't Hide From Me (Luc)
Don't Leave Me (Claudia)
Out of Time

A Billy Jo McCabe Mystery
Nothing As it Seems
Hiding in Plain Sight
The Cold Case
The Trap
Above the Law
The Stranger at the Door
The Children
The Last Stand
The Charity

The Wilde Brothers
The One (Joe and Margaret)
The Honeymoon, A Wilde Brothers Short
Friendly Fire (Logan and Julia)

Not Quite Married, A Wilde Brothers Short
A Matter of Trust (Ben and Carrie)
The Reckoning, A Wilde Brothers Christmas
Traded (Jake)
Unforgiven (Samuel)
The Holiday Bride

Married in Montana

His Promise
Love's Promise
A Promise of Forever

The Parker Sisters

Thrill of the Chase
The Dating Game
Play Hard to Get
What We Can't Have
Go Your Own Way
A June Wedding

Kate & Walker

One Night
Edge of Night
Last Night

Walk the Right Road Series

The Choice
Lost and Found
Merkaba
Bounty
Blown Away: The Final Chapter
He Came Back

The Saved Series

Saved
Vanished
Captured

Single Titles
Loving Christine